AVIARY SLAG

AVIARY SLAG

Stories by
Jacques Servin

Normal

Copyright © 1996 by Jacques Servin
All rights reserved
First edition
First printing, 1996

Published by FC2 with support given by the English
Department Unit for Contemporary Literature of Illinois State
University, and the Illinois Arts Council

Address all inquiries to:
FC2
Unit for Contemporary Literature
Illinois State University
Campus Box 4241
Normal, Illinois 61790-4241

ISBN: Cloth, 0-932511-91-0, $19.95
ISBN: Paper, 0-932511-92-9, $11.95

Photography: Bill Jacobson
Cover Design: John Lindell
Book Design: David Dean

Produced and printed in the United States of America

For my uncle, Charles Myran, M.D.,

who spoke English with crows

As with any definitive reference work, the present form of this book derives from the strenuous efforts, scientific to sexual, sometimes just numinous, of more individuals and organizations than could ever be thanked, or even correctly identified. So for now, thanks to the reviews and anthologies in which some of these pieces first appeared—*Bomb, Exquisite Corpse, Hanging Loose, Avec, Black Ice, Goodbye to the Twentieth Century, Asylum Annual, Fine Madness, The Illinois Review, Caliban, Columbia Review, Denver Quarterly, The Swansea Review, Global City Anthology, New Works, Five Fingers Review, Rampike, Colorado North Review, Intimacy, The Salmon, Furious Fictions, TO, Bandicoot, Alea,* and *No Roses.* Thanks to the the Yaddo and Camargo Foundations for time, sea, the gull in my teeth and a measure of calm. For calm, thanks also to Laura Rosenthal, Joe Wolin and Arden Reed. Most translations are mine, but the credit and blame must go to the language.

Contents

LIMINARY NOTICE (OPTIONAL): CONCERNING THE VITAL STUTTER OF CROWS

There is a world and above it a world
      below it likewise a world   etc.
There is there is a way a way you
un voyou   away you!
you, you
         you have
Words.
With words. (Words.)

Put, the, vulture, in, the, cage!
Efforts are made
a calmness reigns
in spite of all a calmness reigns.
Honey!

      —Alphonse Tache, *Le péché chez
      les bêtes*

When birds were men, and men were birds....

      —New Caledonian tale, from
      *Bulletin de la Société
      d'Anthropologie de Moncelon,*
      series ii, volume ix, p. 613

Welcome to the aviary. Here you will find most of the varieties of exotics you have come to admire and worship and perhaps even frequent. It is true that none is available in the usual senses or non-, ringed by and ringing with knowledge and use, but this should in no way diminish your visit. Your visit can be rich, can "pull wherewithal from negation," can engender effusions, ablations and drainage, can pop. It can be something you describe, later, in words—"The birdsphere surrounded me fully, there was no space for breathing, I clutched"—or in dark little lines—say, a drawing of one of the features. (For non-obvious subjects see index.)

At the beginning you will find a display, demonstration, and discussion of flight, with reference to the drug, marijuana, which is used here not so much for its effects, which are often annoying to both user and friends, as for its conceptually alliterative properties. It stands for LSD, cults, Plato well grasped, and all other scourges of America's youth's parents' mindblowingly dopey instructions to America's youth, often mistaken for America's youth itself. In one of those psycho-physical metonymies reputed more common in biblical times, the pot plant is used to make rope, and burning it in its unravelled form in one's lungs or nearby helps burn tethers to inherited lemons of thinking, at least in one's teens (later it just makes one smarter or stupider). Each tether torched, the artery it bogglingly still is for others can, for one's entertainment and progress, be riddled and pickled and served up in dizzying flourishes of once well-woven errors. (This is often mistaken for cruelty.)

In the second part is the story of life after rote on a different road, tether hemp frayed and burnt, worry defrayed, with curtseys and scrapings to certain completely certain ideas in complete disrepute, and salutes to the forms of living that depart from those commonly catalogued as fulfilling the wishes of numina best. None is endorsed, some are proved vital, many are licked up and down.

These first two parts outline the whole of this world—life hindered and not, hinged and not. The third deals with issues of self and its mysteries, and in the last are more potshots at arteries, suddenly whole again forms of imprisonment, not torched or melted at all.

If these four prefab chunks don't do it for you, several additional sections, pamphlets, proofs, manifestos and tracts can be formed by reading the index for topics with three or more entries, or by adjoining like topics. Reading the state-name stories could be good preparation for a cross-country trip. The stories referred to by "Androgyny, usefulness of," "Annelids," "Bug-eyes, attractiveness of," "Cleopatra," "Fraternity boys," "Heterosexuality," and so on could form an excellent prom-advice pamphlet. If your faith has been flagging, read up on "Hasids," "Mists" and "Recycling."

There is guaranteed to be produced, somewhere, in one of the sections native or composite, at least one of the chancy excesses that dreams, truth, and flight are consigned to be made of forever (unless, of course, you're still hoping for *Lebensraum*).

A brief word on history, that necessary evil. There is a history to the birdhouse, of course, but it is far beyond the scope of our thinking, let alone this discussion. There is also a much more manageable little history to our interest in birds.

The head curator speaks: "Birds are quite a bit sillier even than fish. What is sillier than a bird? Nothing. Yet birds have determined my life.

"When I was a boy of eight, I went to visit my uncle psychiatrist, whose mynahs were the shame of the family: he was sure he had taught them to think, or rather to tell him about it. 'When the world finds out,' he told me, 'I'll be as famous as Darwin, anyone.' (*Was* Darwin anyone?) Then, demonstration: after telling them it was my birthday, he asked them what day it was, and they squawked out some sounds that he translated to mean that they knew.

"Later, he sold them.

"In the early 1990s, another researcher, Irene Pepperberg, proved beyond doubt that her parrot could think. From her office in Tucson, home of the Biosphere, Jane Goodall's chimps, the Garbage Project, the Multiple Mirror Telescope and Norm Austin, she declared in full view of the bird-behavior community, on which she and her family depended, that her little gray bird had the cognitive abilities of those chimps and dolphins that others had managed to befriend and prod for their secrets just as, in the legend, the first or so white Americans had with *their* subjects.

"'I am sad,' the parrot confided to her one day, as she left it for a routine medical check-up, 'and I don't wish you to leave me alone.'

"If I could, I would name this the Charlie Myran, M.D. Arearium. Or perhaps, since he died right after Dr. Pepperberg unveiled her parrot, I would name it the Myran-Pepperberg Construct and Archive, or the Myran-Pepperberg Ornithopticon. But I can't, any more than Caesar could name his Rome, or America's natives America. In any case it doesn't exist.

"Mph."

If in the course of your visit it becomes apparent that indeed, there is no aviary here after all, take comfort, this has been studied. There is, to be precise, a two-inch layer of inky green matter covering the ground where, previously, the grandest living archive imaginable could always be seen. This matter consists of near-equal proportions of all those qualities which founded the "substantive base" of the structure—the thoughts, ideas, errors, dilemmas, and perverse little resonances which allowed the mere object to stand. If you scoop up a handful and sow it among your turnips, you may obtain within days a perfectly-scaled little replica of all civilization, there in the turnips. Don't.

In the air above the inky green matter, the sometime stuff of the birdhouse: its cargo, now loose, yet uncertain of what to do without walls and fixtures and curators, and therefore preserving the concept of same so adroitly that visitors are still often misled into seeing the thing. But there is no thing—nor, strangely, has there ever been. There are only ideas, and part of the charm of the aviary is in its heightening of this fact through the partialness of its masking.

There are those who consign themselves to this puddle of birdhouse for fairly long periods, the way moonstruck medievals would crouch in the bowls of miracle fountains till their leg-muscles started to atrophy, claiming it made all life singular, distinctions vanishing into the black hole of each jot and tittle's feral uniqueness along with their cramps: there are truths, these touched would declare stretching back into shape, but not as we think of them, nor ever will. For many, this was an issue of comfort, for others a matter of mystic something or other, while yet others were finding something specific they had dropped at a fairground some decades before, or would drop the next.

The alert citizen of the abstract will indeed note that truth, unlike beauty, can't always be seen, in the usual sense. Though there is such a thing as negative capability, it is most often while falling asleep, or being shocked out of hiccoughs, or being conked, or whatever, that the whole picture shows up in some form. Then one says "Yes, there is something here to wrest me from damage," or "No, I will no longer fluster the vitriol of my dearths," or the like, before submerging in sleep, gratefulness or unconsciousness.

Some experience this moment as lunacy or powerlessness, which is why it so rarely occurs, but the curators call it "ideation compaction" and see it, as do the parrots (from whom, if truth be told, they obtain their ideas and phrasing), as a means of salvaging life from the slag (modified from the parrots' more elegant but foggier "means of dredging the dogged," or "bogged," or something). (Despite differences in vocabulary arising from different milieus, curators and birds are agreed on most things, including these concepts, and on the goals of the aviary: loosening of strictures, effective if muted revolt against ways of thought and vocabulary imposed by milieus, deafening of the shapes of constraint into shapes, mere this and mere that, rather than shapes of constraint. The parrots call the malleability of reality that makes this possible "the flightiness of all factualness," or "the lightness of all actualness," or something like that.)

In events, one thing will occur regardless of neighbors, and another will never occur, all strife to its doing a lark in its eyes; by a different token, each thing will roam to each other regardless of order, but the cause and result are of one's own gazing, like Australia of the Australians' singing.

This minded, you needn't start anywhere in particular in your visit, any more than history had to start with an apple, tablet, or cudgel. Nor, as through history proper, need your motion be influenced by any arbitrary decoction of lines such as these, or those to be birthed from exchange with the index; like the order of living events, lines are a matter for plotters and fishermen, not for the quick.

You should steadfastly ignore all this chatter, in fact, and randomly wander, perhaps waylaying one of the parrots briefed to discuss, without any traces of vanity, most any subject concerning their new cousins, the apes and the dolphins. While the trainer is pleased to announce the parrots' near-complete grasp of the research, cranial size prohibits presentable discourse on all other usual subjects, and visitors attempting to ask about traffic, clothing or other hard matters of localized interest will be asked to depart. Questions pertaining to the absolutes of philosophy have proved surprisingly easy for parrots even without education, and are therefore allowed, if not exactly encouraged.

But don't get caught up with those beaked cassette tours either. Just scratch on the walls, demote ceilings, eat floors—slobber on something, if slobbering helps. If you find yourself rethinking what-not, don't reach for your pipe, just go on and do it, and think also of health, boys, gadgets, malaria, grunge, and especially that tongue depressor of knowledge, the sameness of life.

TORCHINGS OF TETHERS, POTSHOTS AT ARTERIES: A PICKLER'S GUIDE TO THE HIGHWAY

There is an animal whose name is *Yadu'a* ["Known"]... which grows like cucumbers and gourds from the earth, to which it is attached at the navel by a kind of big rope which comes from a root. The *Yadu'a* is like a man in the shape of its face and in the shape of its other [sic] limbs. No creature can approach it, for it tears everything to pieces and grazes everything around it as far as its rope will reach. When they come to hunt it they shoot at the rope from a distance, and when the rope breaks the *Yadu'a* instantly dies.

—Shabbatai Bass, *Sifte Khakhamin*

BEACH TRENCH: A FABLE OF PARENTS

I see at last... the great wild aviary, the sea as gullible as a bind-weed.

... My shoulder can now go to sleep, my youth come running. It is this alone that should furnish immediate and working riches. For there is one pure day every year, a day that digs its marvelous show in the foam of the sea, a day that rises to the eyes to crown noon. Yesterday... the shark and the gull did not talk to each other....

... Make every assumed end be... a feverish forward for those who stumble through the morning's heaviness.

> —René Char, "Le requin et
> la mouette"

A great horde of belles-turning-punk arrives at the ocean. The ocean contrasts sharply with their 'dos, velveteen and attitudes of benevolence, with each feature in a different way. There is something profound about this, notes a parent on the boardwalk. There is something notably important about this, thinks a boy on the boardwalk: something I will want to remember long, long from now, when I have my own belle-turning-punk surely charging similarly along a similar path as any one of these belles-turning-punk in a horde arriving at the ocean. That is the boy's first thought about this.

The belles have arrived from Des Moines.

They break into a fisty gallop. The ocean is very much there, licking the punctilio from the belles' upbringing, rampaging also in a certain way, buffing the sweat of their voyage into a sheen hardly distinguishable from the standard lacquer of walnut or fine oak, welcoming them to its unusual clutch.

The belles' particular frenzy is so extreme that their legs have surpassed the gripping function of sand and begin to enjoin upon it a very convincing rendition of dig, so that with every split-second step the horde goes deeper and deeper into this lip of the wild sea. Wild sea, ever an only slightly lessening distance from the horde of belles! Wild sea, not hosting at all the bathing extravaganza perhaps envisioned by each of the belles in turn somewhere between Des Moines and the sea, thinking "Sea, wild sea, what will you hold for me? Huh?"

The hole gets deeper, and with it the belles, who are charging at high romp ever higher, going deeper and deeper into the beach, that beach of a different constitution from the dirt of Des Moines, o dirt fled from wrathfully, dirt. The sand has enveloped the fastest of the belles so that nothing shows save puffs from their dynamo enthusiasm, puff puff into the soles of the next-fastest belles, who are also churning into the sand, much faster than the belles behind them, who are also, of course, helping to make this hole in the beach now fifty yards deep.

O deep!

The parents on the boardwalk are somewhat surprised, but see this as all in the plan, perhaps of physics. Many have cameras and shoot with an anticipation of futures that is roughly commensurate with the belles'. Many of the parents' other offspring have disdainful, jealous looks, but many, like the thoughtful boy, look towards a future full of cycles and elemental repetition.

In the sea, beyond the trench of belles-turning-punk, are an army of shadow punks, bobbing in the surf, one wave after another taking them up, down. Many have fixed their bobbing gazes on the parents beyond the trench, who photograph them along with their daughters. Remarkable column! one parent will exclaim at home in Des Moines, much later, noting the grey mass of rebellion in the sea. Much like a part of our own history! another will exclaim.

Yikes, the thoughtful boy will think. Yikes, and not unlike something terrific, grey and deathly, bobbing up and down in the sea. I am very afraid, and yet intrigued. Perhaps, the boy will think, there is some way to contact that mass from a flying machine, perhaps a helicopter, and perhaps I will do so, will be one of the ones who do so. Perhaps I shall one day speak with punk, the real grey mass of punk, out there in the sea, in the surf, in the waves, bobbing. Perhaps in the meantime I shall study the great blue science of oceanography. I have heard it is good!

DELAYED-REACTION COLONIZATION *IN ABSENTIA* OF A
FORGOTTEN ISLAND

Poultry. Energetic madam of Iwo Jima is fond of poultry in its edible manifestations, those which do not take away from the furtherance of the poultry race. Eggs she abhors on moral as well as tongue-aesthetic grounds, but her credo is not a violent one and these problems are private, private to her holdings. Her holdings are not vast.

Mouth. Madam's mouth-position is not the mouth-position of brilliance, to be sure, and neither is it American. Madam holds it inscrutable and spicily near the exit-zone of propriety, there where land holdings form a muddy and not entirely volatile bulwark against the ravages of the difficult fierce. The difficult fierce are ten of her less tractable brethren.

History. The tension of this story arises from madam. Madam, energetic madam of Iwo Jima, holds within her domain the island's *umbilicus mundi*. In one plot grown over with unruly life, angry vines, on an almost phallicly protruding mound of hard dirt, is the umbiliform, aniform manifestation of the greatest American nation's visitation in a dangerous year for this world. The men, and women, of the settlement do not adorn the Hole with sundry tokens of gloating respect. They do not remember the happenings that led to the kindling in the earth of emptiness four centimeters in width and twenty deep. They do not bedeck their hair on certain days with special products of their mills and factories and chemists, or chastise children for puling a fierce, malignant puling on this day of days, the cheerful day of our world, the glen-perfect candor-day for everything dug deep in the bowels of our hearts. They do not smother the Hole. They do not coat it, or adorn it, or glide their angel-smoothed limbs over the earth so enticingly cleft with one gentle dimple to form a pocket of—as the arms, the thighs glide asking "up-here?"; up here the gloating, the cheer come tumbling askingly down to the still perfection of this angry moment. They do not.

Charles. Charles tries on an anklet, another anklet, is wearing his mother's anklets. The masses scream adoration for their warlords, this is the day of woe-coming, but Charles is placid, adoring only the silver on his adolescent feet. Handsome with anklets and hair-beads and sash he looks out the window, well-versed of course in the manifold calamities the masses cry from their splendid perches on the shoulders of each other, aspiring to vertical prominence there in the sweat. But he turns away and finds a book on madam's table, the island has learned to read, Iwo Jima is literate, Iwo Jima has the literacy rate of the United States, and he reads, Charles reads, he reads of bombs and cruisers and stationary and non-stationary targets on land and sea. He looks at the pictures of ships and mountains, and there is one hillock, and he knows why his mother has kept this book. American soldiers at Iwo Jima.

Mound. Charles is fighting through the underbrush, he has divested himself of the feminine stuff and replaced it carefully, he is angry and determined without knowing quite how or why. He claws the vines and finds the splendid rise of sun-burnt clay, nearly brick, a good ten meters high. He climbs and climbs and there, where he remembers from his days of puling, the hole, the little hole his frightened little arms used to reach down into once in a long while. The same. He understands.

Telephone. Charles installs a telephone and orders dishwashers, bicycles, hairdressing kits. He arranges the hair and clothes of his brethren; even the difficult fierce patronize his fledgling attempts. He bravely unveils the Hole from his bicycle. The island succumbs.

THE CAT-WOMAN LUNGES, HORRIBLE AND MYSTERIOUS, AT A LITTLE PIECE OF LINT THAT HAS BLOWN THE WRONG WAY, ONTO TWO EXPOSED WIRES. A NANOSECOND LONGER AND THE PLAN WOULD HAVE BEEN OVER TEN MINUTES TOO SOON, BUT SHE IS DEFT, ATROCIOUS IN LEAPS, A MAGNIFICENT PITCH FOR A BALANCED DIET. THE BOMB IS SPARED! AND THE CAT-WOMAN SITS, NOW PENSIVE, PICKING AT PEBBLES IMBEDDED IN THE HESITANTLY REGAL CONCRETE OF AN AGE OF NEW WORLD POSITION. SHE IS IN PAIN, OF COURSE: GREAT THROBBING ACTION AT THE TEMPLES AND GUT; HER EYES AS ANGRY. SHE PREPARES HER FEINT.

"The glow of atrocity in the public eye has in no way compensated for the lack of rounded solutions," Mark says. He is pacing back and forth, in a way that usually draws his students' attention. "The world explodes, settles back, and crumbles into hard-packed dust. Is that, the plan for stars, to be the paradigm for all our future endeavors? the continuation of suffering in a new, supercompact rendering?"

"No sir," says Tony, who is myopic. "The lands of necessity shove up the boundaries of the continent of home to give the man on the street his lip. A lip he needs, by the way, to keep from oozing into the sea. This lip is bound to save our world."

Mark takes off his glasses and rubs them with his shirt. "Tony," he says, putting them back on, "we do not in this class adopt the professor. We speak in our own plainsong. We do not twist the fabric into hopeful shapes. In this class we are quite alone."

"Yes sir," Tony says angrily. He is terrifically angry at himself. So is everyone else in the class, except for Becky, Rhonda and Mike, who are staring out the window. On their faces, little smiles, archaic. They have the air of men adoring a flag. All this for several seconds, only, the seconds after Tony has spoken. Then Becky, Rhonda and Mike look at each other.

"But no matter," says Mark; "we all have days of atrocious simplicitude—and I use the contruction advisedly." He looks at Tony, who undergoes doubt. It is appropriate doubt, Mark decides, and continues. "The revelations of desire have precluded our

leaping into fascisms with impunity. Though several have tried."
"Hitler, Reagan, El Atroz."
"All have tried and none have failed—but all have paid the price. Their nations have paid."
"And siblings, descendants, believers..."
"Nations, Tony."
"Whose words, Dr. Fipp? Whose groaning, astounding plain-song?"
"And siblings, descendants, believers. Very well, Tony." He looks over his glasses at the class. "Now can we... What you looking at?"
The class is gazing as one. Tiny archaic smiles on many student faces. A cat has ambled in! Mark picks it up and holds it dramatically away from his nose.
"How did they come up with *you*?" Mark asks the cat. "You rubric of countless countings and legislative motions, shallow breath at Whitsuntide..." He inspects the cat's paws.
"Sir?"
The cat's paws consist of some pink, some blackish digits. "Obvious strange thing," he says, holding the cat at arm's length and looking into its eyes. "No nature could have determined you. With your freaky digits. Imagine," he says, looking at the class, "how difficult." The class doesn't respond. He takes off his glasses. Oh, for heaven's sakes. The class is looking as one. Looking towards the window. A symphony of boredom. "Perhaps," Mark says, "there is something interesting out there?
"Perhaps!" he says, and screams, and drops the cat. The class, cued, panics. Confusion grows, a bell is pulled. In the window, face of cat, two big ears. Standing on feet. Eyes alive.

THE CAT-WOMAN BENDS AND BEGINS TO PREPARE HER SURPRISE. HER PAIN DISAPPEARS AS SHE AFFAIRS HERSELF TO MATTERS OF CURRENT AND JUNCTURE. A MUSCLE CRAMPS: SHE STRETCHES AND BENDS, STRETCHES... SHE WORKS, THE WIRES ARE BETTER AND BETTER ARRANGED. SHE LOOKS IN TO CHECK WITH HER VICTIMS, WATCHES THEM YELL. YELL AND YELL AND YELL: SHEER HORROR! THE CAT-WOMAN BENDS AND PREPARES HER SURPRISE.

THE DREAM OF THE CLASSICAL TAILOR

My friends and I are sailing through some beautiful pennants and such. My friends, like me, are built of three thousand mitres each, resembling poorly made up beds. The pennants and knights and arrogance through which we are flying putter up and down louse-ridden alleyways, consuming themselves in an orgy of betrayal—betrayal of neighbor, conduct, nose. As we fly through them, we describe our reactions: "Terrific." "A bit of malaise hindering posings." "Masterful dismissal of everything so apparently cheesy in this, the life of a previous majesty." "Awe-like."

Some of us breathe the air of Sardinia, taut with mists different from these mists of unkindred flushings, and others of us the air of our other homelands—homelands further from here than Sardinia, further than Egypt itself.

Egypt: land of vast men with total ideas.

The pennants, knights, arrogance and betrayal through which we are sailing do not nod to us, do not anchor themselves in our flanking, do not breathe for our moneys. They amuse themselves with up-and-down futzing, linking the cobbler with tarts, the mustard-impresario with his only adultery.

I call to my friends, who, like me, resemble dignified but messy beds in flight. I say to them, loudly and with poise, "Prices are moving but we are beyond their concern! Facts are accosting our punch with a certain *controlled substance.* How does our punch react? In the drag of a wink?"

"Enough," my friends call back. I tilt my head as they argue about my intentions. I am, after all, just like them. I do not cause ripples, befuddle my stalwart munching of progress with image glee, slit masturbation. I am friends with all comforts, lick their shins. What can I mean? intend?

We continue along, the trappings of former amber lifting it out of control and into a future of blocked picks; stumble stumble stumble, and earnestly we consider a nation of honest lifers, laughing it up with the moody cloistered, coughing bereavement into the handkerchief of stranded royalty. How are we to demon-strate whatever it is we are obviously here to demonstrate? Some of us are coughing bereavement, after all, others are cloistered, others are full of axe-miffing guffaws. How do we keep the metal sticking to the best of its crimped allegory (swords, ploughs), the monks describing modes of plasticity, the dead not happening?

It is all this that disturbs us and also, interestingly, renders us flip as we sail through pennants, knights, arrogance, betrayal and scenery. If we could only concentrate on the pennants etc. If we could slumber with mollusks and deal moments from a clipped androgyny. No such luck: we are complex, interesting, doomed.

Somewhere far away a mist arises and describes itself to its father, who wishes it proud voyage with a purse of distinctness and a pat on the tic. It wends its way through the stippled math of this heart of splendor and finds us shredding paper at a café while the headwaiter snacks on a bazooka. The mist describes itself and we breathe it in and soon return to our fine, earnest seekings in the lands certain mists will never understand.

THEY ARE HULKING YET ELEGANT. SMOOTH IN THE RIGOR OF THEIR DESIGN. SHINY AND EFFICIENT TO BREACH A BARRIER NO DISHWASHER COULD, BETWEEN BEAUTY AND FUNCTION. THEY ARE AMERICA, ASSUMING POSITIONS. FORCING HERSELF THROUGH THE GAPS OF A FORGOTTEN IDEOLOGY TO STAND FREE OF THE BRUTAL UNCOUTH AND CONTINUE TO CLOSE THE PARTED EYELIDS OF DEATH. THEY ARE IN NUMBER TWENTY, SHINY AND SERENE, MAJESTIC GROWTH ON AMERICA'S FRUIT: THE MEN OF KAPPA PHI ALPHA.

Mary passes comptroller Hugh with stride of white tile morning, saluting the glorious Abernethys. Mark and Priscilla Abernethy are chief gamers on this project. "Priscilla," says Mary in devilish tones, "there was a burst in A-32 at 0500, there was a burst involving I don't remember plutonium or uranium, one or the other substance, they are both terrifically toxic but as you remember A-32 is a bat in a tire."

"A problem in the reactor?" says Priscilla.

"Generation," says Mark.

"Of toxics," Priscilla reminds him.

"Yes," says Mary. "Yes, it was very ridiculous, totalling only some milligrams. There is no need to mention..."

"The efficient autocracy of the plumbing."

"We have the essential tools, also, you know, my love."

"Priscilla," says Mary, and Priscilla smiles.

Now Mary must dash for her notes. There is a matter of adjustments. She can tell that two men are worried, they are standing so bent and unsupple at the 1x4 plate window. They must be worried, Mary decides, over perceived lack of adjustments. She taps her notes steadily as she approaches them, until they see her upon them. "Only one more thing to adjust, gentlemen," she says, and they bow uncomfortably. Synchronicity is not the dish of engineers, and seldom do they understand the eyebrow.

Mary stops dead in her tracks. "Mr. Galapagos!" she exclaims with solicitude. "Are you ready indeed? this morning?"

Curly "Winsome" Galapagos has a complexion of corpses or ash, with unhandsome freckles and innumerable lines. Mary alone is not bewildered by his face and manner, and he has found through her a deep talent for the Busy Doctor, which now happily infects his every hour. As soon as he sees Mary this morning he realizes he's been gazing at Caroline Boff, whose projects have never ceased to excite him. Caroline is headed for the comptrollers' nook, in her arms a sheaf of essentials. "Mary," "Winsome" says, "you can kill yourself jogging."

"I know," Mary says. "If you're fat." Neither one is.

"Or even if not. People die."

"Also eating salt," Mary says.

"I know. The samurais used to eat salt, to die."

"Then they'd go jogging," Mary says, with a self-effacing wink.

"Not like our men," "Winsome" says with a nod.

"Right," Mary says. "Our men would never kill themselves."

Suddenly the clock is ticking. Mary picks up a wall phone to order the final adjustments. "And the burst?" she hears. There is an air of majesty in the air. "We're fifty feet off on this one," she hears. It is too late to change it. She tells the group.

"Where's that put 'em?" asks Caroline Boff. "Chemistry?"

"Chemistry 105B or C," Mary says. "If my estimate is approximate."

"Who will tell them?"

"The man in the coonskin cap," Mary says.

"With the epaulets."

"Drinks too much."

"Has woman on his breath, every morning."

"Disgusts our boys, in a way."

"They could find it titillating?"

"I didn't say that."

"But the critique in your tones..."

"They could look at things a little upside-down. Find the breath of working-class woman..."

"Attractive. Quaintly, as in the nineteenth century, young men had 'wander years,' to explore and notice the world, appreciatively."

"Saying certain candid things to prostitutes."

"Only to be rebuffed, garrotted by the distance implicit in that social relationship."

"Do prostitutes care about the physical form of their clients?"

"An old question. You should be over it by now."

"Caroline."

"Mary."

"Ladies!" Curly "Winsome" Galapagos makes wild sweeps at his wrist with his eyes and opposite hand. "Opening gates! And you critique the milieu!"

It is at this point that most things happen. You open the gates, you can find yourself with a situation more complex than before. This time, it goes well. The men are aimed wrong, of course, but fifty feet can be corrected. The enormous steel of the hangar doors is folded back on itself and the pride of America's peacetime efforts becomes an aspect of the classroom environment.

"Look!" says Mary.

"Look!" says "Winsome."

"Look!" says Caroline Boff.

"Look!" says Priscilla.

"Look!" says Mark.

Mary rips the top sheet off her pad and twists her shoulders slightly to the left. "Look," Mary says. "They are rebelling." Everyone smiles.

THE MEN OF KAPPA PHI ALPHA SMOOTH BROWS, SHUCK NIGHT-TIME FRETS ONTO DRUNK, STAGNANT SHOULDERS AND KICK PEBBLES INTO THE SCRUB. THERE IS A BALANCED WARNING IN THEIR GAIT, AS THREE BY THREE, IN SEEMINGLY RANDOM ASSORTMENTS OF SPACE, THEY JUMP THEIR SHOULDERS AND ELBOW THEIR ARMS IN THE GENERAL DIRECTION OF THEIR PROGRESS. "SOMETHING'S WRONG," ONE SAYS. BUT IT IS ONLY A MATTER OF FIFTY FEET.

A Lot of Us Were Wearing Head-Dresses

I was the plastic explosives man—the guy they called, you know, four-thirty in the morning the bell rings, a mischievous little pat-a-cake kind of head of state goes faith-down as they say, friends-a-bobbing-in-duct-tape-fondles, and everything topsy-turvy because of this pat-a-cake kind of asshole, yeah. That was the guy I was, the guy who dealt with the plastic explosives end of the whole transaction, you know, when you're dealing with ending the friends-a-bobbing-in-duct-tape-fondles kind of mischief asshole, there was lots to consider and I was the guy, I considered some of it. Plastic explosives.

Now plastic explosives is a lot like mixing mortar on your own mother's neck for interring your father, if that's the kind of psyche you're stuck with, or like choosing your friends out of a chamberpot. In both examples you're dealing with a lot of care to be taken lest you end up massacred one way or the other—your font-of-all-loving-kindness a hardening design in the entranceway (if no one ever comes in that way, otherwise in the cellar), your life a bunch of hang-tos and mildewy underwear worship. Similarly, with plastic explosives a great, great deal can go very wrong so that no one gets paid save in jetting-through-flesh kind of action on the part of material which, to you, had been a complete and total stranger.

Much of the material, so you know, is not really plastic. Sure, the stuff that goes in you is plastic, but that's only because it has to be hard and the kind of stuff that could very well go in you. The rest is whatever chemicals explode, like in hand grenades, fusillade-repellent sort of barricade boomers kind of things, and even bullets, but only special bullets—your regular vast-issue army plugs cheapen your life a lot, sure, but compared to the stuff in my plastic explosives—well, even Auntie Mae's weirdest cherries don't glance off these barnacles.

Anyhow, I was the guy who spent a lot of time getting ready to do something or other with plastic explosives, which I've described, and finally something came up and though I'd been restless and even fretful, often, asleep on my couch, hours and hours each night full of fretfulness, this night that the thing happened was like the one I used as an example above. You know, four-thirty in the morning the bell rang and Sharpie's there, turned out a leading man of the important political parties was scraping by with a bit too much hard-earned cash and waking all the neighbors besides—and I who resent the status quo as if it were my own mother! Not much needed be said and I squashed this, perfected that, mimicked that, and put together your so-prismic ball of future in nothing flat and gave it to Sharpie, who looks like one of those guys who kills you after he's gotten what he needs just so no one tattles, but he knows me, I'm too gullible and energetic to tattle on anyone, but there was a second there, me handing over the plastic explosives and Sharpie just standing there looking cute like you'd expect of your killer in that cute killer way you'd expect, when I wasn't all that sure about the next few minutes. I have to admit. But here I am!

Anyhow, plastic explosives is a rough business and there's a lot to it that ordinary folks don't want to get involved in, quite rightly, but it's my line of work and it's not so bad if you ask me. Not so bad.

L'ABBÉ MARTIN SERLES DE GINGRICH SPEAKS

This one is about the time I was an aristocrat in the revolution. They were giving me pointers on dress and decorum but I thought it would do to involve myself more actively in the cause of the penniless, even name my son "Penniless," and I was wrong because one day as I was wending my way down the tortuous and ill-defined mapwise alleys of Paris a beggar approached me with his friend the other beggar and their wife the third beggar and demanded to know the god of my wealth so they could adapt themselves to its demands because at this juncture they found themselves ill-equipped to cope with even the simplest needs of the human frame, in which they most certainly made their lives as surely as I. I found myself cornered by more beggars until it was unmanageable and to my distress found I had to sacrifice my vows with an unsightly flourish of what I'd been trained in.

Anyhow I evolved a theory of the absolute wisdom of all the races and classes and presented it to the faculty on combined efforts of will and to my distress it was voted down for a great reward they were offering to increase the chances of solution. For by now nearly everyone was admitting his virtual dereliction in the face of the uprising which people took to calling "the heavy arousal" on account of its effectiveness. It was voted down, my theory was, and I had to retreat to the holes of my functions for the next thirty days during which I evolved a better theory involving the whole of reality in a subtle conspiracy to eliminate the grotesque. Again I was voted down but this time with winks and nods that lent credibility to my efforts which I had taken to calling fledgling. It felt like a nightmare but I was committed.

Around this time I got to feeling better about myself and ventured out alone through the dark and tired alleys of a mapwise obscure Paris. My Spaniard friend referred to my city often in his good efforts at correct pronunciation but it is a long and fierce history, Paris, that must not be simplified. I refer to my Spaniard because I was carrying his poniard and foil, having borrowed them from him at Le Ballon Invisible the night before, and that is a story in itself. So I was out with arms and soon noticed a beggar talking to me, a Sri Updike or Cheever or something, and this beggar was telling me tales of alternate byways through the difficult lines of our cases and the talk was enchanting and I turned to him and with deft eye recounted my enchantment upon which he opened up and I was full with the pleasure of my newfound friend to replace the Spaniard and I invited him to my chambers, which I have not yet described, and he accepted and we wended our equally delighted and perturbed way through an unclocked Paris.

My chambers were large for I had accumulated my many treatises and the material I had needed as background to write them. My friend removed his hat and his poniard and laid them at my feet, saying kind things about me but unkind things about my fledgling efforts simultaneously and I found to my illimitable distress that there was nothing I could do to prevent the necessity of forsaking my vows with an unsightly flourish of what I'd been trained in.

Some good arose because I was struggling with ideas of integrity and justice for quite some time and now I found my thoughts flowed freely and I suggested to the faculty a new balance to the old formulations, which to my joy I discovered needed not be discarded but could be subtly held or balanced with the average skill of a generally agile bureaucrat. This time I was rewarded with eighteen glances and three thousand four hundred *louis d'or* which I quietly secured in the vault of the bank belonging to my longtime friend and confidant the honorable M. Denseur Izet, who possessed a ranch and foods to refine the faculties to a metallic whine. With him I finally spent rewarding days and never found myself or my values endangered.

So that is what happened, and the rest is history. Masters, when you are growing along the paths that nature dictates do not forget to pause and look at the piddling human efforts so enthusiastically propounded to you this afternoon, and consider them as lessons. There are ways other than this, but it is important to remember certain things and when such a stricture exists the other ways are more difficult than death itself.

Capitalism

The merchandisers flowed into the central arena and warped a bit of spacetime to make some delicacies, whose uses, virtues and (in one instance) inhibitions they propounded to one another in highfalutin tones. "I'm just sitting on the modicum of recalcitrance *this* fright of a hedgehog transmits to the holder." "You may canvas all tiny reactions and canvas all giant reactions, but you'll never canvas the full range of deeply-felt sympathies *this* food processor brings out even in organized criminals." "Journey far, journey near, but don't journey at all unless you've got Stealth Unaccoutered. Stealth Unaccoutered is not ridic, wan or shafted. Stealth Unaccoutered is handiness standing."

This was intimacy unalloyed!

An actor wandered into the show and declared to the assembled his love for the moment, his desire for rest unrelenting, and his mostly unexpressed hate for The Things That Are Wrong With the World. His tears streamed down to his feet, right past his genitals, which were quaking with all the sundry tenacities of a grand motive. The merchandisers bawled, they leaned upon one another's shoulder and ran solicitous hands over one another's chest and belly, and their tears ran down to their feet past their genitals, which were shifting hither and yon with all the confusions of psyches aroused and unmastered. The actor bowed, shuffled backwards and out, and the merchandisers fell upon one another with tales of wives, houses and heroin.

Then there was an intermission, with the kindest merchandisers standing upon footstools brought by other merchandisers, and proclaiming the meaning of rest: "Rest, that stippled pond. That snowfield caught up in banks like bunched velveteen. Take your rest, good merchandisers, for the needs of the day are upon us, nearly, and something remains to be done." The footstools were rendered back to the appropriate parties. A fine bliss of hominess shot through the bunch.

During the second half, things were returned to their constituent elements by a master disassembler in from the sticks. He knew tires, nutcrackers, galoshes, computers, and the patented essence of farce. The merchandisers ran to catch each part as the master disassembler hurled it into the audience, hurl hurl, not even alerting the audience of each hurled part with his patter. "Gonna snap, crackle, pop, 'cause the din of the mustard's a-courtin' the mousse. Shriek and unbend, freak and relent, there's nothin' but shaftedness here." His beard reached down to his genitals, which had lain in wait for seventy years now; he displayed them for a moment, and the merchandisers oohed, for there was a religious element in all of them.

Then the music began. The music was enormous, there were tympani galore and all manner of beauteous, shimmering trills and mordants in the violins, and a mighty fine pianist squandering riffs on the Steinway as if riffs were replenishable. The conductor had a moustache and tackled the trumpets at one point, launched himself into the air over the second violins and landed smack dab amidst the trumpets, whom he tackled to the ground, bending their instruments into amusing animal shapes which he threw to the merchandisers as tokens of his and his orchestra's affection. He was a devoted conductor, anyone could see that, and the merchandisers applauded with one heart, and something was improved in the spirit of American enterprise.

Finally dusk threatened from the distance. "Ho," said a merchandiser, "if I am not mistaken that is a mass of dusk on the horizon, looming." "Yes," said another, "I wouldn't warrant a nay to that augury." "Ho then," said the first, "it's high time we pealed out of here, no? Come dusk, come dark, as they say." "Come dusk, come dark," said the second, wiping his nose, "but I'm not entirely sure of this particular configuration. Still..." "I know what you mean," said the first, "you mean we are blessed by the lightbulb." "Yes." "Ah."

The lights were lit with some ceremony and the merchandisers gazed into each other's eyes in the new extra brightness. They remained in the arena for hours and hours, for there was depth to their delicacies, and endless uses, wants and even inhibitions that wanted propounding, and only a lifetime for all.

Sexes

"You will have to push on this pedal, and ardently, for the world is without definition and what stump we can fuse it with we invent, propose, design, whistle out, conceive, varnish in, and stick to the fabric of every which way."

"Like this?"

"Yes. You are a woman, a woman thin and brown, long like a cucumber and brown like a sea cucumber, whistling often, gifted with the connecting impulse, willing to put circles and squares in league, willing to join the hub to the cab, the hubris to the bris, making one thing work, the other thing also work, whereas normally few of these situations develop."

"Yes."

"You will push until I tell you to ease up. You will continue to understand this mechanism through me and my arms of glacial stymying, you will see the through bit and the down bit and the swivel bit as if I were seeing them, which I will be, for I am the worker and know full well the deft steel of my cordage."

"Yes."

"Now push on the pedal."

"Like this?"

"Yes. You are assuming the worst of the void, making the swell interferences list like Caravaggio on his futon of papal bulls; you are reckless and yet serene, joining always, joining and never renouncing your clues, like many an Austrian scholar betrothed to classicism like Herod to the Jews; you speak tomes about death by surrendering whole your leg's decisions.... Push on that pedal! Whack it!"

"Like this?"

"You are spindrift collateral, forever argy-bargy in the face of the daft unruffled, but giving the wind its joys. Yes, like that. Your leg, pushing like Greek boys against the plum of their lovers' dilemma, the plum of their lovers' dilemma, and forming essential distempers by lugging sequence from this land to that land, always confounding the systems but giving the rampages lust."

"Yes."

"Now remember to know when the oil is low."

34

"The oil is low?"

"The oil is not low."

"Oh."

"Remember to know when the oil is low."

"Oh."

"The oil surrenders pride in the interest of obtaining conviction."

"I do?"

"The oil surrenders. You merely push."

"Yes."

"Push."

"Yes."

"Push."

Only the Wicked Are Marching
(A Difficult Hour)

Sad Lola, destitute on our show today, could you say something about the quality of the present?

It is bad, the present, but that's because of the chips I've got on my shoulder that render the present, well, all sorts of colors you wouldn't imagine.

Is that so? Lola, would you tell us a bit of the life it's taken you to get here, to this place, to this station?

I've been through a dozen things, it's not easy to say everything because...

I know, Lola, just be a brave proud woman and tell us the things.

I'll say the first things, the things involving my father. An offshore dilettante, he amassed quite a good fortune by convincing others of the value of welfare.

Welfare?

Yes, and he passed himself off as extremely likely to be the next victor in the fight between those in favor and those opposed, even though he was neither.

Opposed to welfare?

No, to the fight. He was brave and extraordinarily beautiful.

Describe him.

He was nearly seven feet in height and his stature convinced a great number of people that he was the one to take over a great number of things. Involving him in some talk on Baudrillard was a task. Some things a girl doesn't outlive.

Describe yourself, Lola.

I'm five-foot-eleven, three hundred pounds at conservative estimate, a landslide in my esophagus every night, a brain for a stomach and vice versa....

And your son?

My son ironclad in his glow of just-pretty, a real nugget in hell— something you might want to lead about by the nose, say, or give to the neighbor to assure goodwill.

Very nice! And me?

I am going to slaughter you, render you, quarter you, dissect you, give you no stridency in the channel to life, put guts of you down on the floor.

That is so! Tell me about your parentage, Lola.

I thought about this a lot one night. A thousand of me sprang from the bog, menacing homeowners, flaunting a cheesecake of suddenness and the throughway collapsed and a flight of dissemblers aroused them till more, more, more were the numbers of same treading same, and so on.

A genial flit! Perhaps we can go on to sturdier measures. How would you prefer the thoughts of the audience—cozy or wicked?

Wicked, as it is only the wicked who march.

Yes, folks, it's only the wicked who march, and you're tuned to "Only the Wicked Are Marching." Next week: flaws in the creaturely studies of Blake.

Pallet of Awe, Missouri. A fragrant young medicine vendor arrives at the house of Chuck and Prima Mitterand, laved of late in the sweltering Rio del Sol Aniformo, the River of Sun Unfolding. "You must harness your wants and clip your frenetic limbs at the joints," he says, lest they consign themselves to a similar pattern of laving forever. They purchase manuals and hide behind stable doors thinking, thinking, wanting but not appreciating, listing to grandeur, listing to pride, and thinking, thinking, thinking.

Soon they divorce and own up to the random in life, the passacaglia mischief even in lounging, and purchase rewards commensurate with their feelings of envy. Chuck learns to be a boy and befriends other boys and soon they are all achieving stasis by the wayside as Prima drives by enhanced by the surgeries most elegantly propounded by such creatures of dredge-and-suction as the Drs. Guigui Priff-Mews, Lambertine Shrovemanshipt, Panical Beef, and Horseblende Puriah.

Claim To Muffledness, South Dakota. A treasure of molluscs unfolds in the sweet summer twilight, invading the township, grinding against the bumpers of favorite cars and less favorite cars, causing a ruckus to be dismissed only by Red Hatcherado, a fantasy man whose briefs send the molluscs reaching for flags promptly lowered by councilmen wooed by the brightest of no-nonsense gift-shop owners; the molluscs, bright in the stripes, leach themselves into flavor-dust and are sprinkled on Howie Muscularity, who earns such raves in his new, mollusc-flavored form as will definitely shred into asphalt-brick-flesh-concrete strands the town of Claim To Muffledness, South Dakota—tomorrow, when Howie stands up.

Ankh Putsch, California. Eighteen-wheelers sand this reporter classically, dutifully mending his flick-of-an-eyebrow dismemberment with the *totallest* worm of the muddy season, the annelid *Corrigens corporis*, a worm you *don't*, however, want to season by humoring it in a truckstop ribs place, for it will then regale you with its nudity, shucking itself lengthwise into rawest strips which will harm you, downright harm you, in front of your dutiful trucker friends who have only always meant to adorn you, you know. This reporter checks out with a somber wave at his new Asian boyfriend,

Toast, and settles in for a ride down the saddening stretches of laid-low canvas vendors who litter the coast like so much argent math.

Disco, Utah. Free beer entails the release of unquestionably false myths of origin into the slick, crime-happy skies full of each other hovering, staid, in those skies, dressed in khaki and wine, absorbing said myths with a puppy-dog look for a long time, intent on the curvature of one another's earth, which one can perceive just barely, in the distance, with the use of seventeenth-century instruments of navigation and perception. Do you see it? When you first saw it, were you surprised or did it glide into your life like a leaflet into Hiroshima, like a flutter of leaflets into Hiroshima? How many of you were there at the time? Were you discrete? How many now? Discrete?

Only the Wicked Are Marching
(A Difficult Hour)

Candy, a virtuous celibate woman who ties stool together in hours away from her father, is here to teach us some things. Candy, what are your names?

Candy Celibate Creatures Manganese Stult.

Candy, offer us in all innocence the true derivation of that, your surname.

Stult?

Stult.

Stult is the blossom on seven gables, a thousand on each actually one growing high and the next just as high, a lot of blossoms coming out of what you must know is in the Southern climes just terracotta, and even cotta the terra is nice to the blossoms. There are flowers in my land, flowers everywhere.

So the stult is a blossom.

Stult is my name and I am very fortunate to be here.

Tell us more, then, about not only your name but the other aspects of you.

There are great, vast stores of truth in the monkeying with the sorrow of knaves—get one, tie the knave down, make him shout, make him screech, then you get truth because in all honesty he isn't talking about just any burgher, he's *screeching* about what you might not want to hear, the plain dismal facts of the factual ways of just where he is; and, as I said, that might be too much, but there's power in knowing some things and that's what I'm all about, Candy Celibate Creatures Manganese Stult.

That's nice, that's nice, we're rolling, we're coming in for a big old excitement...

And there's solid truth to the ways things work, that too is what I'm about, and there's fact in the homing-in way of the thing, and virtue and love and this and that. But I don't want to get in the way of attraction to love or to any other thing there might be in the great, very attractive dance you're living in, the big to-and-fro, the heavy massage of dilemma into the stuff of harsh purchase on stacks....

Stacks?

The stacks we might speak of, otherwise, as things that help us through...

Help us! That is a good idea, no? For we are lacking, no? Tell us, Candy, we are lacking? And if so, why is everything so sheer and metallic these days? Are we wicked?

Yes, we are wicked, but then you know, it's only the wicked that march.

Yes, folks, it's only the wicked that march, and you're tuned to "Only the Wicked Are Marching." Next week: variety and desiccation.

The Great Lay of Spain and the Frugal Inquisitor of the Primitive Mind

"Hello, attractive young female of the sparse subcontinent, Spain. (She is very hot-blooded.)"

"You, my exquisite, ungarnished beast, are the key to my freedom from cum and the well-swept brothels of the breathy matadors of my youth, which, I must rasp, is still going."

"(She is very hot-blooded.) That is interesting to us, dear girl. Tell us more about one of these breathy matadors in particular. Tell us anything—any matador facet or aspect—and any matador's person, moreover, will quite do."

"There was one, Humberto, serene but huge, with a dimple in his left cheek that could hold a stone as large as itself, and Humberto reeked always of breath that he breathed, which was breath of the drunk, having drunk this or that which sent him into a fit, always, of knowing himself pretty well, which was unusual then, self-knowledge, always people were going around with a decided purpose, yes, sure footfall and graceful contorting, but no vision into the head—but that one, drunk, could see that, for example, he lacked the stability to do things but only because of demands placed upon him by neighbors who didn't care much for him— 'whether he lived or he died,' as a singer of America sings— that without such demands, Humberto would thrive and have stability and even more thriving thereafter, and he knew, too, that it was he and his cowardice keeping him loose in the shovelfuls of pig iron that were coin for the Neighbor seen as grand aspect of Neighbor, and Humberto could hardly live with that and would fly into rages, and me he would come to sight with his eye into mine, one eye, you know, into another, and I so frail with the eye of a girl he would look into in that manner of the selfless cowardly matador, a terrible manner, really, and this would all make me quite nervous and often my breath would shorten and not from that action of excitement that shortens the breath as one approaches the house of companions where one will have the hand with companions, etc.—rather any shortening there was due to the situation of small being faced with a very real matador, and so on and on."

"You know, of course, that we are American, very rich, we can buy you out of the state of Spain and take you to Idaho where you will learn about life in the modern world and its processes, you will be cared for, you will be cared about too moreover—many things! one thing after another, caring.... This is not just a suggestion, a hint, an idea. Perhaps we can talk, first, about some of the other matadors."

"I am too eager to go to America, exquisite ungarnished. It would solve a great many errors plaguing me lately, errors of ill comportment in the face of advances—often it is very nice to have hand with companions—and in the great country of your departure I would talk and talk about any matador there might come to your mind."

"That would be nice indeed. (She is *so* hot-blooded.) But you know we are studying the great notions of the primitive mind, a good many thoughts about that that are not for sale, they're very precious to many people who live in America, your future home, and we really would like you to think about things in your life for us now. Right now, not really in future America."

"I am really disappointed, I am sinking, it is making me clutch a matador to my breast and be lanced by the matador's gaze as well as his notions of future serenity—you make me very sad!"

"Well, for one who disdains future serenity you sure are missing America."

"Not for serenity do people seek America. Rather because of blunt-brained despair."

THE CAT-WOMAN SITS BLAND AND UNIMPRESSED IN THE CENTER OF THE STARTLING ARENA. ON THE RISERS ALL ABOUT, MENFOLK JEER AND TOSS CORNFLAKES, SPAGHETTI WRAPPERS (THIN), AND MEAT TASTEES OF PORK, BEEF AND JUNIPER HEN. THE CAT-WOMAN RAISES HER POLKA-DOT-TED ARMS AND CALLS FOR SILENCE. THERE IS SILENCE. IT DAWNS ON HER THAT SHE IS THE ONE IN CONTROL (NOT THAT SHE HAS DOUBTED IT: STILL, THERE IS A MOMENT OF INSINCERITY WHEN THE FOCUS IS REVISED). THE MENFOLK JEER WITH ONE MOUTH: THE CAT-WOMAN CUTS OFF THAT MOUTH. THE MENFOLK, MOUTHLESS, GURGLE ENDLESSLY IN THE GATHERING DUSK.

"Malcolm," one says, "in the beginning of after the beginning..."

"Not that again," Malcolm says. "I'd rather hear the dupe-and-bunny tale this time, Stew."

The dupe-and-bunny tale... Stew does not know the dupe-and-bunny tale. "The dupe and the bunny rose higher and higher in the echelons of middle-level marketing at Sears & Ellen until in a fit of panic sequesterers arrived and doomed the caboodle to..."

"Breakfastlessness." Stew does not like it when Malcolm interrupts, but Malcolm interrupts quite often. In this case, he wonders, is it real? Has Malcolm actually stated the story in its wrapper, that Stew has filled at random? For Stew this was quite an experiment. Stew did not know the dupe-and-bunny tale.

Elsewhere in the environment, the women, Marjorie and Smith, growl at simple paintings, earnest efforts by stagnating youths. "He is fifty-four," Marjorie says. "Earning his millions by sticking up nerds."

"It could be worse," Smith says. "It could... Huck..."

Marjorie understands. She is hoping for better. "What do you mean?"

Smith smiles.

Marjorie does not understand.

THE WOMENFOLK SHUSH THE MENFOLK AND GATHER AROUND THE CAT-WOMAN. BLAND AND UNIMPRESSED, THIS LATTER DISPLAYS A WINK. FIRST, A WINK: THEN, TWO

WINKS. THE CAT-WOMAN OPENS SOME PARCELS, DISPLAY-
ING HER: COMBS, BARGAINS, DUPES. THE WOMENFOLK
TIDY THEIR FAST WHITE SKIRTS. THE CAT-WOMAN DODS
THOSE SKIRTS AND THE WOMENFOLK, SKIRTLESS, TIDY
THEIR LEGS IN THE GATHERING DAWN.

SADNESS-CAUSING PIECE
Morality Play

"Kiss me, sir."

"I will not. You are very wicked, and come from a terrible nightmare of sticky brutalities whose only advantage, I believe, was that they led to your brother's renunciation of malevolence, your family's only heritage."

"Oh, sir. What has all that to do with you and me?"

"You are wicked and I will not do the wicked in any way, on earth or in heaven, or live with the wicked or swing the wicked even angrily or even connive for the wicked's bereavement, or love the wicked or detach myself from my affairs for the wicked's sake or pledge my troth to the wicked even for the second it takes to light a torch under said wicked's effulgence, or groan with the wicked in height of mastery or earn the wicked's approval or approve of the wicked's wickedness or live under or over the wicked or consolidate my firms with those of the wicked or congeal under the wicked's eaves as ice or fuck the wicked as you, wicked, would have me fuck you."

"That is not true, sir. I would have you earn my respect by being my love and good conscience and seeing the effects of that love and good conscience on my often wicked behaviors. Lessening them."

"I would not want to engage in much truck with the likes of your wickedness. It would not do me to squander my soulful ambivalence on wickedness grave as yours, gaudy as yours, extreme as yours, plenty wicked as yours. My soulful ambivalence is not wicked and it is what has undone the past of the nasty things in the species and improved the good things and earned for the species a sort of okay place in the present that I think will last for at least as long as my soulful ambivalence finds its companions not in the ilk of you."

"Sir, I have lips that are great for kissing and are not wicked."

"Not wicked? How? When the whole of the beast is wicked, are not the lips wicked too?"

"Not wicked, sir. Nor I, essentially."

"Wicked and family wicked and wicked with pets and wicked up high and wicked down low like a bat and wicked consuming things and wicked ascetically and wicked damagingly to the commonweal and wicked benignly on occasion and wicked very much."

"That may be, sir. Kiss me, sir."

"It would be hard stool in breadloaves were I to kiss you."

They part.

"I wish to speak to the merriest of the friendly wives you have lounging about. I see they are many, and friendly—perhaps you can pick much better than I?"

"It is easy for me to pick, because I am large and also friendly myself, friendly as Ganymede flitting through sorrow, friendly as turnips in cheese."

"Then which wife do you choose me to speak to?"

"The wife of your choice."

"How can I know, being of sour disposition all my life, a toad, terrible?"

"This one."

"This? She is tiny, and fragile; I am afraid I will wig her out or snap her in two."

"Then this."

"This? She hulks over me like a vast fire brigade. I have evil intentions for those who would be unto me like a fire brigade unto me."

"Then this one here, discreet, pleasant, robust but not hulking by any means, certainly placid when you get her listening to her favorite songs, intelligent too."

"What songs are those?"

"The German Cavalry Join-In song, the Taut Grunge Beleaguered song, and others of that ilk."

"They are not my favorite songs."

"Then this: she has a thousand virtues and one of them is always knowing the time of day."

"What time is it, woman?"

"Another is not the gift of frivolous talkativity which virtue you seem to esteem as is your right so sacred I'd die to protect it disagree as I might with you, your thoughts, your person, your life, your value, your danger to the infants, your danger to the ponds, your intrinsic luminosity (lack of same), and your terrible habits dooming the race of men."

"Another woman would be nice at this point to see if same might become me."

"This one."

"I'll take her.

"Now I am walking home and there is a strange breeze in the air.

It is very enjoyable, after a fashion, for it reminds me of customs and habits long out of my mind—by that, dear wife, I do not mean I'm out of my mind—but it is very cold and I feel I might die from the chill in the air and if you do not provide me with warmth I might blame that on you.

"I see you are holding my words in the highest esteem. The look on your face reminds me of a very intense look that the Arabs use at times to signify pleasure intelligently taken. Perhaps that is good, and perhaps there will be a very long to-do, our lives a-squirming, our piecemeal manitous lingering over a happy fire, and God glimmering shadowily in the gloaming.

"I am cold! There are solutions to cold, I have heard. One is to practice the great Eastern sciences. The other is to retreat into special Western warmths. Oh, there is a third, and that one is very nice, perhaps that is really the way for me. Onwards! Onwards!"

WIFE. THEN, EVENT.

Odyssey, heterosexual

First things first.

I christened my wife "Invulnerable" and trundled her down to the bay. There we stood a great long while singing to the ocean liners ferrying whole nations of confused, ardent poachers from one great untrammeled, unwrecked continent to another, ours. Here they would swing past my wife and me on into lands unexplored by either us or them, shooting the this and the that with the caliber of their choosiness, loud, and we still singing, perhaps, on and on into the vast night of their indeed very nicely grounded assumptions.

We stopped singing and stared out into the bay in silence, the ships, the ships fairly loud and rowdy, and then I looked at her once and laid her, back first, onto the water and gently shoved her with a toe of mine and observed her unique and gorgeous, that great bobless scurrying into the water of that body of her, my wife, a glorious scurrying to make me weep in transport of knowledge, aesthetic, and there my wife was, and I mounted her there and directed her into the bay so that waves might part and she and I sail some great distance onward.

I noted my wife, that her health was not good. She was leaking great flows of mentholated effusions from tooth and nose, it seemed, and I merely shivering on stomach deck listing from the sheer mess of our strandedness remote as it was from pharmacist, surgeon, or friend.

I tried, oh, to steer her, wife, "Invulnerable," down through the corridors reserved for the huge shipping vessels our country has used to transport its valuable forms, as well as, glorious, its values without form, formless, to others in the world who have few skills like ours, but the wakes from the vessels destroyed what plentiful ease had been my wife's and mine there in the bay, despite distance and disease of my wife, and we rocked and listed a good bit before sinking half down to the silt that I knew from my studies must lie at the foot of these waters.

And then the rest of the way, all the way down.

There, of course, there was much, much wet, and my wife who was leaking in need of a surgeon could not be distinguished as leaking, but the menthol leaking distinguished us from the tasty versions of flesh which the gargantuan sharks which prowled these depths had a fondness for, thank God we were not that tasty version of flesh—my wife, in any case, saved me!

It was ages before we were rescued and when we were it was ages before we were thoroughly dry and the age being what it was yet ages more before our city recognized us with a plaque for "Healthy Bonanza of Survivability Today." It was good, the city expressed, that we lived so well and so long and in such a historical timeline, not unlike that of the city, not unlike that of the country, this great ardent flimflam blimp of a country neither you nor I know the end of.

Our apartment was remarkable and one day my wife and I were sitting across from each other at dinner, toasting the veal, encouraging thrift in our future encounters of butcher, damn it, and I got the idea that lands were there for the settling, oceans were there for distribution through consciousness and that many of us, my wife and I for example, while poor, had a right to those terrains so submerged, effectively removed from the feet and soul of us, kept from our tonguings and strikings-off from lists of must-sees.

So!

So I spoke again to my wife of the value of veal: she thought it strange, as we had once already that night discussed the marvels of cow still unswollen with fulness of cow, its taste, but being a fine wife she lifted her glass and it was as I was pouring her toast that I came upon the name "Invulnerable" and gave it to her with the butt of the bottle upon the front of the head, first, and then on the softer parts aft of the pate, and as she assumed the more traditional poses of strong oceanbound vessels my certainty redoubled and the wind built up in my chest and I belted out some great homilies in the key of B-flat and trundled my wife to the quays and we sang some lively but peaceful tunes of pain and joy to those excellent journeyers from lands of merriment to greater lands of untapped death where they might encourage the growth of some fine, fine habits among us. We cheered them nearly endlessly, and then set off on some fine adventures up and down, up and down.

THE ROTE LESS RAVELLED:
BEING LESS THAN A SUM

"She's a Talker," Said Vainamoinen-of-the-Well-Confused-Tongue, Wiping His Feet

An epic of Finnish psychiatry for Neil Goldberg and cat

Steadfast old Vainamoinen   uttered these words:...
"Bear, apple of the forest,   chunky honey-paws!
When you hear me coming,   hear the splendid man
    stepping along...
throw yourself flat on a tussock,   on a lovely crag....
Then, bear, turn around,   honey-paws, turn yourself
    about,
as does a ruffed grouse on her nest,   a wild goose about
    to brood."

—*Kalevala*, Poem 46

"I have longed for you my whole life, honey-paws, have
engaged your freak visage, woods-apple, in those furtive
rompings and stompings down lanes of mind that speak wider
and bolder of love than the keenest sacrifice by a tender-lapped
virgin," says Vainamoinen, big kingly Vainamoinen. "And now
that you're here, I know it was you I was seeing, those years,
bundle, because of your dimples, firstly; next, the signature
whistling   and
whingeing of fortune, the sound of it rushing through brambles
of last year's finessing, wrecking all pretense; and finally the spine
of my lust jutting harsh at my torso, only on sight of you abated.
Your calm figure ennobles the years of my wait, supports my pattest
displeasures with others, every cliche of annoyance become now
fast buttress for this, our union—and I feel a pressure to forebear
further shrinking from shunning the bustling world of men and
effects with its manifold damaging fixtures."

"My bear, my darling,   honey-paws, my beauty,
do not get angry without any reason.   It was not I who
    killed you;
you slipped from a shaft-bow,   you misstepped from an
    evergreen branch,

> your wooden pants torn through,   your evergreen coat
> ripped across."
>   —*Kalevala*, Poem 46

"This opening song of mine is getting harder and harder to sing, bear," says Vainamoinen, burdened by depthless tradition. "I know how you rap the formica, these days, and that makes things just so much starker, the relief more wicked. But this is how it has always worked, continues to work, and may do so always, the skill of men willing. And lest you be shivered to answering lesser elaborations than mine, be clear that my skill with cliche is no fart of abhorrence. There is a strict difference between the stinking of airspaces as mark of disinterest or worse, on the one hand, and rolling the epithets glib as a dysentery from the hard-narrowed tongue. My tongue is narrow, no doubt, and glib; sincerity I angle only towards what I love, and what I love is subtle and weird, like yourself, and thus my love always needs to be angled weirdly. For what is glibness but ellipticities, and what is that, at best, but a roundabout aim at something too strange to bear reasoning with, such as yourself and my feelings for you? Love your basking beneath it, and never let it be said within earshot of you that your basking beneath it does nothing to liven your endless dreary, despised-of-men moments, pudgy-feet. And never, ever doubt the thrust of my apings. All this to say, gold, dear one, that without these formica-relieved addressings of mine you might never know of my yearning. A more modest formula could more easily cover a mean-hearted flatulence; mine, never.

"Now. I would like to suggest, honey-paws, that something is amiss between us," says Vainamoinen, who is as reasonable a Finn as any. "It hasn't been off the whole time of our friendship, so I can't assume it's my killing of you that did it. It could be, rather, the stench of my recent affair with the Countess's leaf-boy from on down the lane, whose habits and lusts are not seemly, I hear, in the bear world; I can only counter that here such ways are *de rigueur* for those who would make a killing of more than literal force—for us, the pressured, it 'lets off steam.' Or it could be my eyeing of other large game—but a hunter, I might tell you, is beholden to shove his craft down the gullet of seemliness, for the village must eat, the toddlers swell, the old folks creak a bit longer, regardless of fondness the hunter may have for one particular trophy.

"The problems we face are thus twofold, and sides of one coin," says thoughtful, logical Vainamoinen: "I must kill, for simple reasons of frame and tradition; and I must make a killing and thus break your heart, for *complex* reasons of frame and tradition. Your troubledness renders this finicky coin."

Then old Vainamoinen   uttered these words:
"Where shall I take my guest,   lead my golden one?
Shall I perhaps take him to the shed,   put him in the hay barn?"

—*Kalevala*, Poem 46

Vainamoinen makes his way through a grand hallway decked with photos of his ancestors, for his family is big in this land. He is giddy with anticipation of meeting the grand-dame of Finnish perceptivity, Dr. Kainulainen. "Hello," says the receptionist. "Dr. Kainulainen is five doors down on the left. She is ready." Vainamoinen walks five doors down, to the door with the little green tassel that symbolizes life's winch, life's grand, alive winch out of murky confusion, the confusion of non-science in today's grimy world. He pulls out his door-rap, an intricate iron bequeathed on a forebear by leaders of Goths, and raps on her door.

Dr. Kainulainen is sturdy, dark, a sheen of nomenclature bathing her slapstick-stock Finn-in-the-library look, which she tries to dispel a bit with a zany green St. Jude. She beckons to Vainamoinen. Vainamoinen shudders. The session lasts an hour; afterwards, Dr. Kainulainen agrees in the interest of soul-besieged humanity everywhere to do me a play-by-play of Vainamoinen's troubles. Out of respect for Vainamoinen, who it must be said has an embarrassing set of attributes, I will not repeat it, but only Dr. Kainulainen's summary:

"People in extreme situations are known to have a recalcitrance about changing. People in cities, astronauts, technicians, seamstresses delivering goods twenty miles, soldiers for God, drunks in lots, United States citizens—and hunters supporting their villages. Vainamoinen has difficulty accepting things into his life that contradict the habitual brutality and murderousness of his hunting world, which includes much of his past, his cronies, his psychic make-up. This difficulty of acceptance would extend, paradoxically, to that which he hunts; so that even though his avidity in pursuing his game is sincere, once he obtains it, has it 'in the bag' either literally or figuratively, his reaction is often one of repugnance—a repugnance so fierce it becomes physically based—like a psychosomatic illness—and at that point, of course, there is really nothing he can do about it without the help of thoroughly trained, completely developed and unhastily accredited experts from the institutes rightly in charge of the minds of our citizenry.

"Now, of course, we are facing the thing that, in Vainamoinen's own words, he has labored his whole life to find. I do not mean to make this object of Vainamoinen's want—let us call it (please take no offense at the impersonal pronoun), let us call it his rug, for in psychic terms it is that, and I do not mean to cause offense thus, or demean it—I do not mean to make this *rug* sound like a problem— forgive me if I do—though in psychic terms, it is—it is something, certainly, that challenges many of Vainamoinen's comfortable assumptions, premises, and operating mechanisms—but of course this doesn't demean it—it would be hard not to evince a certain awe in the face of something so... *inanimate*, as they say, being so capable of causing a major distress in such an important figure as this Vainamoinen, who is, let us say, very large.... In any case, it is the traditional pillows-versus-whips dilemma."

> Then old Vainamoinen uttered a word, spoke thus:
> "My bear, my bird, honey-paws, my bundle,
> you still have ground to cover, heath to clamber upon.
> Set out, now, gold, to get going dear one, to step along the
>   ground,
> black-stockings, to go along boldly, cloth pants, to go
>   ahead."

> —*Kalevala*, Poem 46

I know what is coming. "I have told you, cloth-pants," says Vainamoinen, "that I feel a pressure to forebear further shrinking from shunning the bustling world of men and effects with its manifold damaging fixtures. This is true. And it is equally true that your coming has jolted me headlong from certainty. But at root it remains, in deep, deep ways it is firm and unbending: there is you, fuzzy bundle, black-socks, and there is the rest of the world which, for me, is not you...."

Only one thing remains to be said: while I do not understand Vainamoinen and cannot condemn him entirely, I am only somewhat enjoying my more mercantile life of the last few weeks, and miss his feet, his gaze, his appreciation, his odd, joyous epithets from the speech of the Finns. There is nothing else to be said. But I would like to thank the government of Finland for its solicitude in these matters, its proper esteem for the meshing of this one and that one, and would encourage it to continue those efforts, despite the necessarily endless stream of failures like ours it is sure to encounter.

Classics

"All right, Rex, seven of our youths have trodden to doom in the war zone."

"Which seven, Cort?"

"Burg, Cusp, Derogation, Ma, Platefork, Choices and Swooneroony."

"No loss at all. How many cans of spaghetti?"

"Six. Eechee's, Martyr-o-Plasty's, Plinth-Compare, Sargon and Lovers, Truth's, and Slam-Smith's."

"Since when do we name our cans of spaghetti?"

"We don't name them at all, Rex. It's the varied coups of the slip-up dredgers that name them, Rex. You *know* that, Rex."

"Don't be a wanton, marked-for-jingles orphan of striptease, Cort. How many maidens have trodden to doom in the war zone, Cort?"

"None. That isn't fair yet."

"What ever happened to that one youth with the auburn hair and the lilt to his giggles and his skill with the abdomen?"

"Abdomen Vladek. Conscientious objector."

"Oh good. Perhaps a curtain call?"

"Afraid he's firing doilies for the Mathilda Regiment."

"Funky disease of the potter, you've got."

"Funky drama saving the wine, in the distance, with the guns, and the sparrows dodging so effortlessly, and the wine begging for saving, and every last cloud taking the shape of Mussolini to remind us of the power of the Italian dictators."

"So. Besides tallying dead, what are we doing, this fine homosexual morning?"

"Here's Browner, Rex. Browner, this is your Rex."

"He doesn't know Latin, Cort. Look: he's afraid."

"Afraid of *you*, Rex. Wants to know first if you're human."

"I'm human, Browner. Browner? Do you like being called that?"

"He likes it, Rex. Else why would it be his name?"

"I prefer the name 'Sacerdotally,' in actual fact."

"Of course you do! 'Sacerdotally' it shall be. Now Cort here will show you the graveyard."

"Thank you. In actual fact, I do not withstand graveyards."

"Cort. Will you show Sacerdotally the laundry room instead?"

"No, Rex. Japhtha's supposed to meet us at the graveyard."

"I will grow slowly accustomed to the graveyard in question. I will not falter and fail, becoming as leaves."

"Good Sacerdotally! Good youth! Now both of you, out. I have some interesting investigations to pursue. Investigations involving Churning-Bob Crisping, I'll have you know."

"Come, Sacerdotally."

"In actual fact, I prefer to retain. A little tantric joke. Are you Buddhists?"

A moment later:

"This is the graveyard, Sacerdotally."

"Looks more like a laundry room, Cort. If that is your name."

"I prefer 'Frownmaster' when out of earshot of Rex. That is his least favorite name."

"I see that. It is not hard to see that. Again, a little joke. It is a nice name. In that I am not joking. It really is."

"Thank you, Sacerdotally. This *is* in fact a graveyard, and this is where we must be until Japhtha arrives."

"Is she really due to arrive?"

"Not really. You and I will have to satisfy each other until it is time for Rex to remind us, you and me, that living here is a tale of endless sorrow."

"Yes. I am glad to hear that. I have had several problems because of no getting off."

"Jesus, Sacerdotally, that is a terrible thing."

"Yes. Let us get off, and quickly."

"Please."

Much later:

"Rex, Sacerdotally and I are back from the graveyard."

"A fine time, Rex. Really fine."

"Good youth. Good Cort. Good."

NATURE

The first morning out, Benny arose, stretched, filled his lungs with the air of the mountains, and spelled out the words he had learned the night before.

Jack arose and went for Benny's mouth with his own before remembering that Benny was a guy; he pulled off Benny's shirt and held him from behind around the stomach.

Benny looked off into the forest and thought of the mountains. The words were all there.

Jack reached down with his free hand and made Benny come. Benny sat down and said "Whew."

Jack cooked a fine breakfast of meats, eggs and bread. He watched Benny eat. He watched Benny's stomach eating and breathing. Benny stopped and put on his shirt. After breakfast Jack took it off again and pulled him close. He played with Benny's shoulders and then suddenly stripped him of his pants and socks. Benny looked odd to Jack naked. Jack pushed Benny's shoulders down and walked a few feet off. He walked in a circle around him. Benny had no expression; he only had one when something surprised him. Jack took some rope and tied Benny's hands to a branch above him. He stood in front of Benny, then untied him. Then he dressed him.

They walked for about four hours and came to a lake. There were fish in the lake and plenty of plants. They fished. Benny watched Jack fish. He watched Jack take a fish off the hook and conk it. Benny caught a fish. Jack took it and conked it. They fried up the fish with some plants from the lake; Benny tried to remember where he'd tasted that before. Surely not at another lake.

The lake receded into the distance behind them. The first time Benny, in front, turned around to look at it, Jack grabbed him and took off his backpack and shirt. He gave him back his backpack and kept the shirt. They walked for three more hours.

At sunset they fell asleep. By morning the down was soggy in spots with Jack's come. Benny felt some, moved away and wiped his flank with his hand. Jack put his arms around Benny and laid his head on Benny's chest for ten minutes. Then he kissed Benny on the mouth for ten minutes. Benny didn't react for the first thirty seconds, then began kissing back. After three minutes Jack had had enough but knew that Benny would be disappointed if they stopped now. He knew that Benny was completely happy now, was really speaking.

Benny was really speaking.

They dressed, cooked breakfast, laughed about some things for the first time since leaving. Jack led the way. They walked fifteen miles that day.

That night they made a fire and sat by it for a bit, but mostly moved about camp.

Benny thought about the trees.

Jack thought about the trees. Benny was beautiful.

Three days later they'd gone eighty miles all told. Jack was a bit more tired than Benny and Benny tried taking Jack's clothes off and playing with him and Jack was happy about that, though uncomfortable generally.

When they got back to "civilization," as one or the other called it to the annoyance of both, they did a lot of comforting things.

Over the next few years they took several more trips together, each time living a bit differently, in different ways. Things changed around some but nothing really became anything else.

There are the moments when nothing, not even the taut comparisons between my happy companion's thighs, can relieve me of my slumber. These moments of total non-waking extend for months and in them I will be seen, erroneously, to be skidding down a path of self-abnegation, tack-repudiation, vanity-slaughtering. In fact it is more like repo-man dash that takes over and for these months I caramba mighty through slapdash alleys, crazy-kote dumpster divides, expanses of touchy-feely clandestinity. In there is also a mounting concern for the environment. That environment is as green as my watchband. I love it.

My companion urges me on, at moments like those. He believes I am fomenting drive, classifying the unmitigated. It is all top intelligence to him. He thinks I am dunking home-views in pure moneyed clutter in order to get them a little nicked up.

I am not. It is slumber, the flange on purview that keeps the mystery well within nurturance range, that does not mess with home or beyond. It hopes to clasp itself, lurch voraciously into a creep towards mustard, towards a certain cutting the mustard. It never succeeds, but it slumbers on because always it is hoping to do two things at once and one of those things is already there. One of them is voracious, the other is not. There is something else too.

Eventually the sounds of testy groundbreaking tickle me out of my dump and I pound the asphalt, harder and harder, a sackcloth bonanza, a total skid, and the moments go fluttering out the library window till I, I, I can't remember the names of my lumbago pals and I cry so loud and honkingly that the librarian excuses herself from some pals to come at me with a dirty popsicle, which shrinks me into a thesaurus of kinship relationships, and everything is okay then at times, and slowly I become happier and happier.

No. Just kidding.

Primate. Metabolism: gunky. Loses water in a violent way, on occasion—severe loss of brain fluid may be occasioned by impetuous restructuring of skull. Normal achievements: poor.

"Heads are turning, heads are turning: loss is weaving fearsome malice through this head of mine, mine, through this head of mine."

We embolden the authorities to carry out whatever corrective measures are deemed appropriate. As we prosper, so we dust our lips of cloistered malice. Repeal the flights of this young rebel. Dust his lips.

"We are on the chain gang, we are on the chain gang, we are losing fast, fast, the high-accounted gains, gains..."

Mark and Andy fret as they sit, sit, sit. Mark moves an angry hand across Andy's, Andy reciprocates with slaps to the thigh, thigh, and Mark is left vulnerable in his hostility.

Here is the story that Mark told Andy that night:

"Once there was a chargingly handsome young man, he had lips and hair and even arms of the fiercest sheen, there was nothing between God and his stomach.

"Once there was also a fiercely beautiful young maiden, she had lips and hair that charged, arms that tore relentlessly at the shade in your eyes, and a stomach of no small accounting." ("Hey," Andy said, "hey.")

"The young man and the maiden were made for each other and they became one. They knew one another. For seven short years they delved in, splashed out, came in, hung out, loved in, lusted high and low, lowed loud, crashed short—till finally one day the young man's cow developed a case of syphilis.

"'Hey,' said the maiden, 'hey, how come the cow's got syphilis?'"

"The young man said he didn't know, but his voice cracked. The maiden exposed her tender breasts and began a speech. 'By all that is holy and/or loveable, my darling, I beg you, the poverty of our farm is not such that... The ways of our neighbors are no... We live in an era of... Darling, God cannot be fooled by mercenaries.'"

"The maiden, in other words, was no stark fool."

Mark looked over and Andy was sleeping; he planted one smooth kiss on his shoulder and closed the book. Andy in one movement heaved up and onto Mark.

"Except for a hint of your *tendencies* to the fore, I'd say not bad."

"Andrew..."

"Straight boy."

"Andrew," Mark said through his teeth, "the advantage of a girl is that she's lighter. Also a girl is less prone to violence. That is my experience. At this moment you should be a girl. Usually you're fine"—in a heave he threw Andy off his chest—"but today you're a bad boy of a poo-brain."

"But baby, why, if you know I'm a misogynist who can't stand the thought of a woman's nudity, do you go boom on my sensibilities?"

"You're a dork."

That night they lay side by side and slept. Then Mark went to work and brought home a cinnamon loaf and some beef. Andy was an excellent cook. "I have the appetite of a breaker of necks," Mark said.

Perfunctory rousing of the hurts. "I am not going to cook or speak unless you tell me you didn't mean all that about the girl last night." Promised muteness not upheld. "Or just give me a fucking token, glorious."

Mark plants a smooth kiss on Andy's shoulder. "You little faggot." They have a sense of humor, this is true, and they heave their differences onto it and truck it through the kitchen and out the back door.

The boys, the boys lie down and eat.

We raced around the street in little circles and then dashed off to the corner store to buy something and then eased into "Poppy" for a ride to the laguna where we understood something about the creationists.

We ate and discovered something about oysters.

We went home and discussed various things and looked up and down each other's body and got to the point of having less and less clothing on and then stank up each other's airspace with the smells that come from human nervousness and then fucked.

We fucked until quite late because it was the first time either of us had fucked and we were curious about it to an extreme that wouldn't let us up even though it was unpleasant from the start and more and more so with every passing minute. Oh passing minutes! Would that they might pass more quickly and knowledge be absorbed with much fewer of them passing! That way we might live as in a century of progress and only manageable foreboding rather than a century of total despair every second and an earnestness unbecoming a race of excellent creatures.

We got up and fixed breakfast. We made toast and eggs and bacon and sausage and orange juice and milk and coffee and V-8. Then we went to a coffee shop and sat around like junkies expecting only each other's eyes. Each other's eyes were forthcoming, on time, always.

We got into "Poppy" and resounded across the beaches and hillocks around our community and expected a lot more out of them than out of each other.

Several of the books we had read, it turned out, were admired by the other.

We got into "Poppy" again after a good while in nature and headed to a library, first, where certain things turned out to be true, and then to a restaurant where we sat around for a while before the waitress was really there and then she was just pretty horrible and we wished she had never turned out to be there. Sad us.

The food, too, was not up to snuff. Sad subsnuffage.

We went to an exotic encounter between men, three, and a roomful of various types. The men were extreme in their contact with all versions of literary how-do, and the roomful were extreme in the genius of noticing. Many things passed by us at that reading and there was nothing between us, it seemed. We were as total strangers, which was just as it was and nothing much different.

Lost as we were in that mood and situation, we were never so bent by the unnaturalness of being near each other but not entirely on and under each other that we forgot to look normal. So that each, in fact, was enthralled by the apparent command and steadfastness of the other, enthralled even unto forgetting his own guilt, and the thing was furthered and much was going on at that point and later.

Later we went around and around and considered the houses (many) and the diversions (many) and looked at each other and ambled over coyly to the house most in question and there looked again at each other's body because that was protocol. Then there was a sullen garbage. And the garbage got better and then there were pig squeaks and that was hot. And *this* was a really great thing.

GOOSINGS: A SAGA OF PROSTITUTION
Capitalism

Bo was looking for money. Elaborate money, in trunkfuls. He was dissociated from his own buttocks, that was his problem, and money could cure it. With money he could find a contact he had lost at twelve, when inflation was running wild and many of the banks feeling troubled, at least publicly. With money, his buttocks would be him, his buttocks would anchor to him with the strength they had always lacked, and he could anchor to them as well.

Jersey had money. Jersey came from a family of cat-savagers who, in their years and experiences, had amassed enough money to buy a house in many of the most pleasant vacation spots on the globe. Jersey himself was a cat-savager, and thought that Bo was especially beautiful, this morning, in the sunlight.

Despair for his buttocks! was especially plaguing Bo this morning, and to a cat-savager his archaic eyebrows and saddening mouth must have shone tremendously, this morning. Bo knew how to use a saddening mouth. In Bo, there was no question of how such things could lead to money.

Jersey and Bo went home, to Jersey's house, which became Bo's home for the next five years as his body filled out, his buttocks acquired tinges of immortality in Jersey's photos, and Jersey had the most thoroughgoing enjoyment of Bo's enlarging musculature, which was most tremendous, as it would happen, in the buttocks.

Many of Jersey's friends were impressed and would come over naked to enjoy the knowledge of their friend engaged with such an endeavoring creature as Bo. Bo would endeavor with these friends as with Jersey to remove everything—the past, the worries, the pretensions—not only because that made them feel better but because then Bo could have the comfort of a template and catalyst to bring his former life back to him, a life before anything, when he had longed for anchorage to his buttocks but also when his surroundings had given him cause for thought about himself and he had had the leisure to reject almost everything.

He could not reject Jersey nor, really, his cat-savaging past, nor any of Jersey's friends, their equipment, their connections, their ideas for him, nor any of their midnight habits which sometimes counteracted his now long and elaborate development of buttock-connectedness.

So finally Bo did what any earnest, progress-loving eigh-
teen-year-old would do: he stuffed his bag with some tremendous designer shirts and put on some jeans and marched out into
the warm August night, where however he was mowed down
by the Apocalypse which, much as the Apocalypse is wont to
do, savaged everything, uprooted everything else, and vapor-
ized Bo in a single omnidirectional flash.

Jersey and four of his friends, in the basement, lived through the
Apocalypse and enjoyed one or two more good times before the end
of their luck sometime later that year in a cornfield accidentally
entered for purposes of examining corn and recapturing memories
of important events in the distant past.

Criticism

Diligent, the young master applies his strokes to the canvas. One, two: soon the canvas is covered with the foot-thick deft strokes. They form, in his mind, some sort of bird. An eagle. No, a condor with a vulture inside. No, it is an eagle after all. Or is it (and we are shocked) the head of Louis Freier, the haberdasher?

The young master decides not to work in oils so much. They hinder from his canvas, he asserts, the natural balance of life, because of life's horror-vacuous tendency to avoid fat things. He walks through the deep snow to the butcher's, where a set of pastels has been waiting for him since his sixth birthday. Placed there by "friends of the family," they long ago dried to crumbling bits of gaudy hue. A deep and protracted disappointment ensues.

(All this while, the young master ages. He is now seventeen, strapping.)

A plaster bust is asserting its shape beneath his hands. "Plaster: the miracle for our hands," he says. It is a portrait bust of Caligula, the great Roman. It arouses sympathy from the Carl Rothbergs. "What talent!" they say. "My oh my, you could be really something someday." The young master, seeing only the pessimism in these statements, reacts with a moue.

"My son," says his mother, "what is this moue which befalls thee?"

"Oh mother," he replies, "pry not into others' moues. If you must know, this is the moue of eternity, the moue of Schopenhauer, Plato, and Nietzsche: and life must be formed by the master. Seest thou, or must I weep?"

"Behave," says his mother, but in truth she is giddily inconsolable. She wishes to return to Vienna with her genius son, and little can be done. A trauma ensues. In short order the following scene occurs: Mother and father sit quietly at home, tending their business. The young master is upstairs. Soon a polychrome soup flows down and floods the ground floor, wetting the parents' feet. The soup recalls Jacob's coat. Madness ensues and retroactively aggravates the mother's trauma. The cards predict a brilliant future...

... which straightaway begins. A famous, jolly and lecherous artist comes to visit. He is led in the front door and up the stairs. There, surrounded by tableaux, sits the young master. Much taken aback, the old artist gives him his studio, declaring himself worthless and deserving of scorn.

Another artist, better than the first, also comes. He is impressed and asks to see more. "I will see," he says, "a good bit more—if you will let me." All agree that this is a good thing, the road to success, paved with joy. "Beware, though, my son," says the second artist, and this is the crux of the book: "It is easy to be caught up in one's own greatness, to not see the art, its value, to be led astray into silly realms, silly realms. Then it is not art, it is silly realms. You must cling to art. Own it. Make it in the beach-sand. You must do that which your heart impels you to do, and in addition you must crucify your parents to merit the name 'artist.'"

The young master is struck with horror. Crucify his parents? Fasten them to crosses? A strange proposition indeed. But if it is necessary...

The papers praise him and his work; more laud is heaped on him in a month than most artists receive in a lifetime. And remember, he's only a youth.

Soon the master is older and has grown a reddish beard and has cut off his sidelocks. He still wears a yarmulke (he is a Hasid) but only out of habit. The older he grows, the less life seems to bother him. He is truly alone.

It seems that this is a rather serious matter, this development, that he is truly, truly alone.

Bobby is yanked, yanked and hurled over the heads of his elders. His elders are sixteen graying men with bad complexions and bad humors. They are often sullen and sulky; this has rubbed off on Bobby, who is a sullen youth of fifteen. Given time, he will grow to be a serious man, one dedicated to certain propositions. Given time, we will see the blooming of his moroseness into an unrelenting need to know more. But all we see, all we know is that Bobby, young Bobby, is being jettisoned over the heads of his elders.

How they got here we don't know. We don't care. They are here. No one cares to know why, how, since when. The sixteen zitty old men are here: they are here. Their heads, from Bobby's point of view, sail, zoom, whoosh past, the epitome of impermanence, but they are here: this we know.

For example: one elder coughs. He has had a lung ailment since his forty-seventh year and is seldom silent. Coughing, ever coughing, this elder causes his peers no end of embarrassment. While old, they do not like to stress this aspect of theirs in colloquia, which are often geared to solving the needs of the young, like Bobby. They have never chastised this elder for his cough, for it is not something he can avoid, nor is it permissible to chastise one's peer if one is an elder: and they are all elders, these men. They chastise youths, who are young and amenable to change. At a certain age, it is true, one loses one's ability to adapt to new things: a fact of life. Age brings inertia: a fact of life. And Bobby, why, he has years of painful development ahead: a fact of life. Life!

The elders are graduates of famous and great schools: the school of pain, the school of joy, the school of error, the school of greatness, the school of love, the school of too-much-triviality, the school of affliction, Harvard, Yale. The sixteen have gone through much and are proud, for they are now repositories of information vital to the continuing development of youth. It was they, once, youth. Now it, youth, is in their hands.

Bobby, Bobby, Bobby. They go about the education thus: with force. Each boy is different. One demands subtlety, one requires blunt thrusts. One needs badgers and boasts, one wants trust and slow growth. Bobby, he needs force. But force: where is it really (now let us look at this objectively) to be found among sixteen (we are graying) old men? True physical force? The ability to wrest things from their perches and hurl them pell-mell to divers states of collapse? The strength needed to unhorse afflictions and yet leave undamaged the boy? It is lacking (we can see that) and so they purchase a youngish man, a weightlifter by trade and a very promising man what's more. A man, therefore, who has more to give than to take, and, we are assured by his repeated assurances, fully in possession of the currently necessary sources. A father, a mother, an uncle, a gradfather: these he has; he is a man in no need of more elders. The elders, sixteen graying men, concentrate on the unfortunate.

The weightlifter, then, has hurled Bobby over the heads of his elders. From Bobby's point of view, the world sails past, this little part of the world which he thinks is the whole world. Sixteen graying heads, sullen, sulky, repositories of much, sail by. Back there he can still see the hand that hurled him: he can trace it back to that beautifully developed body, the lines, the curves. It is shirtless, well bronzed, smooth. From Bobby's point of view it is worthy of emulation. Though his elders have not spoken to him yet about it, he is sure they would agree: worthy of emulation, quite. He will speak with the weightlifter, he decides, and discover his secret. Then he will apply it.

One of the elders has reached a decision: no more punishment. Bobby, he thinks, has suffered far and away enough: his learning has gotten beyond a certain point. It is time, thinks the elder, for a quieter approach: no more jarring thumps, no more jogs and shoves. Subtlety is in order, it seems: subtlety and honesty. No more violence: no more. This elder scratches his neck: a boil explodes in silence.

Bobby is falling, falling, falling. His world is sailing past. He is not old enough for metaphors, yet some are obvious. One of his elders sees a metaphor in Bobby's falling, but he does not mention it. Banal, he thinks. Bobby is falling, falling. He is coming closer to the ground. He is inches away. He is one inch away. He has hit the ground, head first. The whole weight of his body is applied to his neck. It snaps. All rush over to Bobby, all closely surround the corpse.

THE BUST DECISION

I was walking through the house of Gertie and Arvo when I heard them discussing Gertie's career. Gertie, as I already knew, was quite interested in the art of producing busts. She had explored the materials plaster, rock, and cement for their capacities to turn into busts in her hands. She didn't feel good about it, so she spoke to Arvo, who listened as well as he could. Arvo was the most avid of gardeners.

"I must, must, must study busts," said Gertie.

"Yes," said Arvo, "I can believe that that is the nature of your affliction."

Arvo was most heavy-handed! But Gertie defended herself quite well. "I have always been drawn to the bust side," she said. "You know that."

"Yes," said Arvo, "I have seen you examining stone on a nice spring's day, either great works or that sterile patronage dreck—as per the proper mood, I suppose, as per the perfect day for that sort of thing. Why you have even bent over the neighborhood fountains and commented on the cornices, corner of 10th and Lexington."

Gertie sighed. "You, on the other hand, have never appreciated the effort of masters."

Arvo looked at his fist. "I have often thought that masters deserve less appreciation than, say, those who make fierce-enough efforts at improving the lot of the foodless."

"It is not so obvious," said Gertie. "There are only a few thousand souls who can properly carve, mold, and set. The world asks for those souls. They must huddle together in groups—calmly, with just the right degree of openness to the outside, just what must be admitted for fertilization to occur. The group itself must be quite seemingly diverse so as to feel pretty good, and yet must be simple and formless enough in its shared understanding to allow the members to examine themselves rapidly and in sync. This is the life to which I aspire—pure, yearning, adorable. The kind of life of which you could write, 'It is mad!'"

"Are you sure," said Arvo, "you are one of those souls?"

"I do not know," said Gertie, "but I certainly would like to place myself in the midst of such action, and test out my busts, for it has been quite some time since I've known what is right."

"Well then," said Arvo, "feel free, and perhaps you and the people you join will be excellent in the world, and attune yourselves right, and prepare yourselves for the world, paschal hyenas. As for me, I turn up my nose."

Gertie wept. "That is sad, my Arvo, for now, if such is the case, I must leave you, and chase my destiny alone in the world of busts, and that is how I leave you, reminding you of the way it is with me, and with my third eye watching my handkerchief to make sure I do not soil it too many times before my future, which approaches, stretches out in front of me. It is long, the world, and far to the other side. Good-bye!"

"Good-bye," said Arvo. "Be careful."

I was embarrassed!

Perversity,

or

A Less Nuclear Family: A Warning to Youths

Ralph and I, both fifteen, burrowed into the flesh of Jane, who was standing nailed to a door in the style of the clumsy-featured door-nailing Goths.

Her flesh was terrific, and Ralph and I as we congratulated each other jumped into the flow of humanity and wended our fretful but well-charged way through to home.

There we spoke to our wives, who were two, and old, adoring each the glint on a grandson's cheek (cocaine). Our wives were on speaking terms with the other of us, not hers, so Ralph and I had to flex one another in some very odd ways and our relationship grew.

Our relationship grew so that soon we were employing the best techniques, not just the latest in claiming a share, or the widest-held by the many, but the best, employing the best to arraign young girls and conduct them to processes in which Goths were remembered in a lively sort of action way and the young girls often, we noted, regretted ever having set foot in this part of the world, which indeed they were usually just visiting. (The author notes that few prostitutes call themselves prostitutes, preferring any other term. There are various reasons for this.)

For want of more young girls, nearly all of whom we had corrupted to death, Ralph and I turned to each other, svelte tense boys with heads of ideas. First we got naked, then we carved little pieces out of the napes of our necks to indicate brotherhood, and also that we wouldn't tell anyone. Then we got rope and hanged one another because that was a joy and then a girl came by and we had some more fun. It was all giving us more ideas, more and more, till finally dark came and on went the clothes and we found our wives solicitous.

Our wives were good with the soup and made us lie flat as we ate, each encased in a five-inch-thick plastic casket garlanded red whose lid could be snapped shut at the least murmur of difference, never to open, perhaps. The soup was good and fed to us through a tube from our wives, who worked in the kitchen, through rooms of our house, to us, and our clothes got soggy with the traffic of love and excitement, and there we endured for a while knowing soon we'd be free and about, gorged nice now and fresh for a while of seeking.

Our seeking went well and we emptied some girls (new ones, late in appearing) which filled our gullets (a pun that enclosed things) yet more, and the joy in our situation didn't abate till bedtime, when, for want of other things, we entered each other with the whole upper part of Christina's body and hanged each other again with the bedsheets, joy. By morning we were thoroughly exhausted and only the brimming-full cereal of our wives lent verve to our stumblings, ironed them over and let us earn as was our custom a fine, fine breadwinner's wage.

There were difficult things there, winning the bread, a lot of truckling and "shadowing mirth," but soon we were eating lunch with each other, jabbing each other's thighs with forks, doing some burn things too on the buttocks (rayon no good for a lot of things), laughing and all in all stampeding thrust of earnestness.

And then work, more work, till the let-out bell, when we threw in the towel of command and arrange, dole-out and hire, thwack and fondle; at that point much of the story above got repeated, different of course but no less exciting, and thus you may be assured was the way unending with us, and still there is joy, we are lucky and happy and no one will ever tell us to be any different.

THE CONVERSION OF NEW YORK INTO BIRDS' NESTS,

OR

THE PANTHEIZATION OF THE BUREAUCRACY

The idea was sound, and we set to work with one hundred thousand pick-axes, three missives in fifteen million cc's (five each) in false cursive, a few model grandmothers exhibiting traces of Modernist urges, and the wherewithal to garner support among the birds themselves.

The basic theoretical questions had been the ones most intriguing to the average shopper. How many birds would submit to the plan? We already knew the answer, actually, but had let people run on about questions of number, size and range. Some said millions, some said one. The people who said one were interested in the shape of the nest, hoping to establish the kindliest dent in their own neighborhood or even right where they lived. The ones who said millions were ecologists, and were interested in the Hudson, the East River, and the accessibility of grasses. They felt that the best way would be to establish many different levels and qualities, many *ideas* in the physical plan, which would give any bird the greatest choice. A few pointed out that this sensibility gave hearty reception to the one-bird idealists, for each bird would in fact be the only bird to enjoy a certain combination of factors fully.

Would each bird find its place? Would they not do better with even, equal terrain? We ourselves had to introduce these ideas, circuitously, through the print media mostly, in hopes that the ecologists would get a bit harder and stomp out the one-bird fanaticos. This hasn't happened, of course, and we have had to plead issues of money, artificial in fact.

The idea was approved by a thousand of our experts and we brought in the grandmothers to go speak to all the old folks. "Modernism," they would say, "lives still in the functions of our first stabs at total literacy."

The missives were distributed, each of the three versions according to its style:

"Birds being what they are...."

"Many of you will follow eagerly these trends...."

"A year and half ago, in the fall of 1...0...."

The pick-axes cleared the land of its buildings, one by one, and the birdseed, of course, brought in some birds.

Birds of the most variable plumage! Grey, green, blue, red! *Many* birds, with different habits. Some of them preferred the space near the Hudson. Others preferred the spaces on either side of the East River. Many preferred the north parts, many the south parts. Many could be seen huddled in the interior mile of Manhattan Island, while others went as far inland as possible. A few floated on the waters seemingly always.

Elsewhere, in Kentucky, California, Michigan and Iowa, people were energetically noticing our work and hoping for better in their own environment. It wasn't lost on us that we had failed somewhat, but we thought it remarkable enough to deserve more than the miffed strivings of our historical juniors. In truth, Kentucky failed entirely despite a fertile soil. California did better but the stress on variety ended up killing off thousands of birds. Michigan and Iowa roughly equalled us.

Later, men, noticing our work, have described other things to their nieces and nephews.

STILL LIFE WITH DRUGS

THE CAT-WOMAN SNIFFS, COLLAPSES IN SLOBBER. "I'D SAY SHE'S ON DRUGS," A PASSER-BY SAYS. THE CAT-WOMAN REARS UP A DRIPPING HEAD AND GLARES AT THE CURTAINS IN THE WINDOWS OF THE NEARBY TENEMENT—FINE PUCE DOILIES STITCHED ALMOST FLAWLESSLY TOGETHER. THE CAT-WOMAN SQUARES HER SHOULDERS, SNIFFS, AND COLLAPSES IN DROOL. EVERYTHING SEEMS CONFUSED.

Mark and Albert finish the table and move to the chair. The chair is hulking, for a chair, awfully massive in a stern-oak way that Mark and Albert have noted Italian things have. Our workers fret and correct, until finally, gracious though sweating, they've filled in the grooves.

"Now it's time for a little boom, don't you think?" Mark says.

"Why I guess," Albert says. "Though don't you think we should finish the bed?"

"The bed," Mark says, and the two move on into the bedroom.

Graciela arrives while Mark and Albert are fixing the bed. "Looks like a spacious hoe-down," she says. "Wouldn't have dreamt of similar speed in my spankingest dreams," she says. "Now what say we have us some boom?" she adds.

"We noticed the toilet," Albert says.

"The toilet," Graciela says and the three move into the bathroom. Mark and Albert get down on their knees and adjust the valves. Then they fret and correct until finally, pleasant though wet, they've eased the fluids.

Graciela's impressed. "I've got some fine boom," she says.

Mark and Albert withdraw from their suits and sit on the rug. Graciela opens a jar and Mark stabs the crosier. Albert whee-whizzes and studies syringes: "A mighty fine box of these do-hards, I'd say."

"Not precious," Graciela insists. "Just 'that which we lose,' just 'truck,'" she says.

Mark tries it first. It works and he saunters bodily out to the laundry. Graciela and Albert go ahead, find consciousness eased. Mark returns.

The three talk.

First there is some talk about motion, that is by Graciela.

Then there is some talk about death, that is by Mark.

Albert and Graciela hush Mark up.

Albert speaks on truth and the way we admire the truth. He is descended of Aztecs.

Graciela butts in with a discourse on love and how love is all motion.

Then the three ease up and enjoy.

"You know," says Mark, "it's a long-standing falsehood that things die by stricture. For really, people attack bluegills, fishermen don't."

"People attack..."

"... bluegills..."

"... fishermen don't. And if everyone saw...." Mark is happy.

"This is not a bad trip," Albert says.

Mark discourses on baldness.

"You've gained weight," Graciela says, to Albert.

"Not a lot," Albert says. "I've gained *some* weight—not an atrocious amount, just the amount one visualizes easily in the you-live-at-home visualization experience. The you-live-at-home visualization experience."

"Not me to judge," Graciela says.

"I don't either," Mark says.

"Let's fish," Albert says.

"Let's fish," Mark laughs.

Albert laughs.

Graciela laughs loudly.

(At that point Graciela, suddenly quiet, asks the two men to strip off their shorts, which they do, and some attractive mammal-pinning goes on and the three are involved in their stuffs, losing trouble of flat awareness—but a dire yet humble presence ekes out its draught from the bouncing of flesh.

(The curtain falls....)

THE CAT-WOMAN PULLS A FOOT UP, PUTS ANOTHER FOOT DOWN, AND THEN TWO HANDS, AND PUSHES HERSELF TO HER FEET. EVERYTHING SEEMS CONFUSED. "TOURETTE'S," SOMEONE SAYS. SOMEONE ELSE NODS: "PAST-LIFE SINS." "SHE'S A PSYCHIC," SOMEONE SAYS. SHE TURNS AROUND AND AROUND AND HARANGUES THE CROWD. SHE LOOKS UP AT THE TENEMENT HOUSE WITH A SURGE OF SELF-SATISFAC- TION. THEN SHE COLLAPSES IN DROOL.

THE CAT-WOMAN SNARLS AND BITES SOME AIR. THE AIR IS SO FETID SHE CAN BITE SOME OF IT. THEN SHE CLAWS AT THE WINDOWS—CLAW CLAW CLAW—WINDOWS BLACK WITH AIR. SHE STREAKS THEM WITH THE INTERIOR, PURE AND CLEAR FOR MYOPIA PURPOSES, AND LAUGHS IT UP WITH HER GRUESOME LAUGH THERE ON THE LEDGE, LAUGHING AND LAUGHING, TILL THE COPS COME AND TELL HER TO SHUT UP, THE NEIGHBORS ARE PRONE TO REVOLUTION.

Minny and Kath are perverse in their love for their building. One of them loves it so much she will kill the other to prevent her from toppling it with excessive weight up three floors, the other's. She will kill the other by various means, including bewitching of the other's effects, done by tongue and heart in synchrony, loving the moments and hating the other. Boom, boom! go the steadfast entries of the one into time. Whammo, goes the other one's soul, whammo, hitting the pavement like so much backup work.

Candace reveals some horrible secrets to Mo.

"I licked so many of them damned apparitions, lick lick lick, I felt like death for some weeks thereafter. Damned if I didn't kerplunk into zeroes because of them damned apparitions."

"Same will cause you delirium, time after time."

"Same will, ditto."

Mimicry death is quite common in the building, for example among the young men, who die one after another of lethargy, smallpox (sometimes) and brutal misgovernment by Sid, a risible cow of a man in his old age, old, nearly lackluster in many ways, very unlikely to send you for loops through ecstasies of dysfunction, these days. Jaw-Bliss is one of those men.

"I am dead, a porridge of luggings at heart, lifeless and sure of my salve, dead as a crude possum lumbering chilly through woods long cut down by my employer, Sid. That is me, chill possum, still playing, and Sid is inscrutable, lumber forever, only rarely even gypsum in fine-tuned misgiving. Me, again, I am dead."

The building often collapses of its own weight, especially between one and two in the afternoon, when the screams of fetid little panickers will lunge for your matchstick decidedness. At times like those you may well catch yourself thinking, "What a horrible world we live in."

"What a horrible world we live in," says Jan, the velcro Swede who trips this way and that on a sojourner's feast, every day. No one can stand him, not even Murphy, who sings his praises to the UFOs who besiege her waking concern. "Save Jan," she sings, "for he is the trust/ the ill-massaged lust/ the snake-oil bust/ of our forefather Swedes—/ I praise him much."

No one can sleep after most events, and when of Minny and Kath one rubs the other out, sentences are read with alacrity but only the windmills continue to turn.

THE CAT-WOMAN IS HAPPY. SHE LUNCHES ON YESTERDAY'S AIR AND DESTROYS SOME LIMBO. SHE KNOWS SHE WILL NEVER FALL PREY TO THE MISTAKES OF HER MEDIUM, HUMANITY. THE COPS COME AND TELL HER TO STOP EATING AIR, AND TO FALL PREY TO SOME OF HER MEDIUM'S ERRORS, THE PEOPLE ARE STARTING TO READ FREUD. THE CAT-WOMAN LAUGHS CONSIDERABLY, GOES ABOUT LAUGHING, LAUGHING IT UP ON THE WINDOW LEDGE, FETID WITH AIR, TILL THE COPS MAKE SOME THREATENING MOTIONS.

The Conversion Of the Palace

Computers

First we had to lower all the standards. Many of the eldest men refused to do this and had to serve a different function, and nothing was wasted. Then the various implements had to be lowered, shrunk, repainted in special gnaw-resistant paints.

A lot of everything was guesswork: what would the goddam things *like?* You couldn't count anymore on flan or bodywork. The cereal displays of this or that mortification ritual ("In Bombay, saddles wear hats!") might succumb too quickly, remove the user to a shivering over the nothingness of it. That was not the intention! But then even the idea of the emperor not wanting to know his own deaths—might it apply much less?

The cloth was a scream. Just an example for you, the battles between the nylon-touters and the cotton-loyal, the running through halls decrying the virtue of ambling blackly in *that* kind of *fuck.* The swinging around and around! only to bounce back into the next room, shivering badly, being helped to vats of thick argent tea by your latter-flash enemy.

What?! when they marched (marched?) in, flushed (flushed?) from their acme (acme?) parade, their laughter (laughter?) echoing to the ends of the scene—how much, for example, of that echo? A dream-built stream of nuisance/horror/acme or a mild whunga-whunga? If not laughter, correct, then what if their noises to them are like bathroom habits to us? Problem, then, given the walls which we find so elegant. Or what if there are no "their noises"? What if they live with only the other making a dent, being painted only by the flutter of corpses past the derision (??) of their open windows, their past and future a (metaphorically nylon?) mesh of wars and events that increasingly seem to entrance only the liquidity of the populace (or is their grief air, their bulldozing rock, in which case, for example, there will be no rhetoric, and *no social occasions?*)?

The wallpaper, the lights, the timers on the lights, the servants' number and aptitudes, the vanities' allowances, the directness of connection to this or that essentially ugly (?) service, the love that might accidentally result from a floorplan, the floorplan's plan for such contingencies....

Few of us will admit it, but secretly we hate the mice. We feel that if we understood them, this move, the ideology or whatever of the whole thing, we would feel better in our putterings and fights, our sweat and deaths. We would perhaps not feel so much better but we would feel much less at the mercy of the rawness of it all. We would not cry. But they have told us nothing. We have never heard from the mice. The only way we know the mice is from their scuttlings out of the way. We imagine them doing more but it is not easy. We try. We consider whether they will see the insides of our minds and whether we are perhaps already offending them by wondering about all this.

Poor us! Hard work lies ahead, behind. We still enjoy the palace, we like its construction, its intended uses, perhaps fulfilled, perhaps not. We do not know that the mice will be bad. Perhaps we will respect them far more. Perhaps they will be more imaginative and use all the effects of the palace to greater extents and in different ways. Perhaps something will happen within us—different rules. Surely!

We can only observe! We can only live! We will see everything, everything, everything that we can and that will be so much that soon we will be drowning in ourselves, and that will be very exceptional, and then the mice will come in and save us, exuberantly.

We were always shimmying around the outside of the edifice, inquiringly, tenderly rude. We used bungee cords and various kinds of cup which required little pressure for attachment. It was great. At times we noted each other, the firm outlines of one another's thighs, the way one or another would cock his head, the effect of the cold on his belly under the half-shirt. Most of the time we peered into the offices and cubicles and decided things on our own about the way things were working inside.

I was the one who saw Johnny slip. Whammo! I could speak it quite accurately—"He slipped. He put on the cup and whammo, it slid and his arm was a windmill and whammo, he plummeted as the facts attest and whammo." I was not argued with. No one sputtered. There was, moreover, no reason to do so. Johnny was on the other side of the building from me. We hadn't touched each other's equipment; no one had touched anyone else in three months. Johnny had not fallen then. Three months and whammo, fallen. Not my fault.

Inside the building, many people were packing crates with notepads, computers, desks, pens, sheafs of 50 bond, sheafs of 100 bond, letterhead, envelopes, miscellaneous plastic desk-jobbies. One woman was on the phone, so they hadn't cancelled service yet. The company was insolvent, it seemed; we turned that over for quite a while, raising our voices against the northerly blasts. "An affair with fallaciousness and general no-goodness?" someone asked. "More like total nothingness. Absence of anything vital." "Like a lack of control?" "Like the whole shebang of the inner office schtick, compelled into whole office gluten, left whiningly in a purse in front of the CEO's terrarium. What would *you* do?"

Johnny gone, I voted twice. Johnny and I felt it was all the CEO's fault. Someone was there saying that wasn't so likely but the CEO was walking around in there in a dog collar, largely undercutting his defense.

A few other things happened up there. There were wine, malevolence, biscuits, derision, paternity, phlegm. There were massive debts to the host country, mighty forgiveness in tense situations, laughable lurchings in and out of paternity (bis).

Edmund recounted the horrors of matching swingle singers to

their prospective admirers, and we each one of us lip-synched to him as if there were no tomorrow.

Later, we spun some tales that horrified the music-lovers clustering about the beams of hardwood that made the ceiling so interesting to many.

Plaster was invented by nuns. Really. Among the decisions the nuns made those days they were making up plaster was (a) dance with those beasts that forgive, and (b) succumb to the rindpest.

I myself was born in the lower part of the Californian coastline. I was educated at Montessori and later, in Arizona, in public schools of varying density. The highlight of my education was the myriad of shocks I and my mind endured at the hands of the Arizona scholarship machine. Not that I'm complaining.

If you are interested in viewing our laboratories...

The starry night officiates over darkened chaos earth and its people. Darkened earth does not often notice, and in the cities by slaughtered walls surly young things engage in brutality.

Is it good? The constellation Musca adjoins the constellations Telescopium and Pavo. Even the skies have been colonized here. It depends what kind of man you're talking about, how he'll look at the sky, of course. Some mainly narrow their eyes, others mainly scrunch their foreheads, yet others stand akimbo, and some put one leg forward, one hand on hip, and gaze unmoving at one or two stars. These last are the most interesting and will inherit the earth. They are conquistadors, direct yet complicated men who want only what will add to the world. They are ruthless and cynical, awful dinner companions, and one cheers to know that they will forever have to till their gains.

There are people to whom the stars speak with deep human voices; these stand by walls and brutalize others, complicating life. To some the stars sing like glass. These build parks and centers for betterment of others like themselves, and relax on the grass, and drink whiskey at night in high-ceilinged rooms with art nouveau wallpaper and posters of "The Kiss" and "The Scream."

We don't really care about the people to whom the stars represent molecules or the ones for whom they are standards by which to measure progress or sanity; these look at the stars lying down. We care about the conquistadors, who fight the stars, and the angry young men who hear the stars' baritone.

Romancing the Smelt: Self-Colonization, Mischief, and the West

When a sow of vitality sets foot upon the moon of perfidy, it is with the moral judgement of the God-fearing faithful legion that the cradle of God's messenger is reached in the hearts of resiliences and will be repelled by good example in the path of misguidances and cursed 'til the day of judgement.

> — *USA Today*'s own translation of Saddam Hussein's wartime address to the American people, which he was allowed to make in exchange for letting Bush make an address to the Iraqi people

Such a life, oh such a life—how can I compass the fret and the shuffling alarums of rev, of swish? Too many anchors abut!

—Edna Lafarouche in *Anything Goes*

PICNIC WITH THE MORIAHS

First things first. We brought in the bags and laid them on the kitchen table, a rickety affair whose cursus honorum would extend pages, simply pages. Into the fridge then, into the fridge with diet pop and T-bone steaks, tater tots and alloy forks. A promising start, to be sure.

And such was the honor of the day that no one dared absent himself. From miles around gathered invitees, rich and poor, large and small, everyone came. Some brought friends we didn't know; many brought pets much like other animals we had by chance espied elsewhere. No one was unhappy, this was the character of our horde: all were pleasingly joyous.

And there was joy, that day. Johnny Handstand, a fellow Moriah from Halmstead, brought us the human body's versatility, its contortions and lithe twists. For nearly an hour we sat in a circle about Johnny Handstand, watching him contort. Afterwards we fried, barbecued and fried. A good deal of mindless chatter was exchanged that hour, for it is well known that food dulls the thoughts of even the most thoughtful individuals.

Afterwards there was repose.

Then, to a rousing cheer from the under-twenty-five contingent, a chick-bake was begun. Who would be this year's chick? Glances scuttled from woman to woman, causing each in turn to blush and bow her head in fear. Finally the young woman in beige was decided upon; she would be the victim. A promising daughter, she was perfect.

Afterwards night fell and a rousing call was sent up to the stars: "Hulloooooo!" we cried, "hulloooooo!" The wine made its way but vanished before reaching the end; aggravation and contribution ensued.

"Where are you?" Mary was speaking to Paul, the third Moriah of East Dorchester. He was hiding, drunk, behind a hedge, and Mary was having one hell of a time locating him in the dark. Very well, this was a fête, thought Mary, but why spoil it through overzealous adherence to fuzzy principles, principles so fuzzy they had never been formally expounded, principles which, if expounded, might prove to be utterly void of sense? This was a fête, thought Mary, but why ignore the threat of culpability? And she was right, in a sense. This must not be ignored: she was, in a limited sense, right. "Paul? Paul?"

But that is the goal of the Moriahs, after all: to squirm out of handy niches and experience a new level of being, to remove the effects of days of thankless toil and start again as from scratch. Do we succeed? It must be answered that yes, insofar as the Marys are suppressed, we succeed.

In the evening the invitees left. All except the woman in beige, of course, and, of course, the pure Moriahs. How many did we number at that time? It is hard to say. Some would count a hundred head or more, while others would limit us to a score. It doesn't matter. The Moriahs were assembled, and they were mighty.

Johnny Handstand contorted once more, and we applauded. Paul, the third Moriah of East Dorchester, amused us with his tales of the space shuttle. A company of seven produced a small play commemorating the founding of New Hampshire, complete with bonnets and English accents. Were women allowed, you may ask. Certainly. They were not only allowed, they were encouraged. With sticks! they were encouraged, with batons!

Thrice our banter went off-color; thrice did we punish. The perpetrators were shedded for the duration! Elsewhere, it was said, denuding and even torture were common practice; but here, among us, kindness prevailed. For to stick together, to avoid influences, was a prime commandment among us. But as Moriahs, how else could it be?

And then it ended. With a bang it ended, with a bang that shocked us out of our socks and made us realize just who we were. We were Moriahs, Moriahs is what we were.

The Symphony and We
Sullen Oafs

In the Western American city of which we were the suburb there was one symphony orchestra—and we wanted it. We had wanted it for quite some time. Propeter had constantly been citing Mozart's perfect balance of beauty on rigid form by means of flowerpots securely on his head; and Mariangle had often stood upon the trellised arch of the gateway evoking the flutter of violins in full Prokofieff with showers from her own wet sheets, which she had waved mechanically and with a fiendish grin. Our desire for a symphony orchestra was by now therefore quite mature, so when the august chief of the central "situation," as we euphemized it, a man we eulogized as "sheriff," "sheriff" in full control of all the hyped-up misalignments characteristic of our section of the West (bulimia sodalities, paternity suits, McDonnell-Douglas), when that august "sheriff" offered us in our suburb full possession of this Western city's symphony orchestra, behind the "sheriff" his favorites, workingmen, a retinue we wittily bemoaned as the "Voices of Ugly"—we accepted. We accepted, despite the confusion we felt, which would be difficult to describe. We did not dwell on it. Momentarily bypassing complexities we opened our eyes to God and heaven and accepted with a deep panache, which involved the opening-up of our hearts to unexpected boons, and in the shuffle we ended up foul of mood and stagnant of soul, for the bypassed complexities were massing in the hearth and stimulating decay and other negative processes.

But then some moments passed and when the "sheriff" and his "Voices of Ugly" left and the orchestra was milling daintily about the entranceway, smelling the blossoms of our rarest species with the gusto of deep experts, we were overwhelmed with pity and with a subtler emotion as well, and we opened our enormous doors and with some hubbub ushered, ushered, to the darkness of home.

"*Now* what will they fiddle?" said Susan after locking the doors and swallowing the key. Many of us felt kinder and, after darting recognizably hateful glances towards Susan, left our comfort to purchase bread, upon which purchase we returned to hurl it in through the clerestory windows, and our natural relief at having done something was doubled by the calm and gentle shuffling and

European-sounding appreciative yelps which issued from the orchestra, which we heard through the doors.

"Heard through the doors!" you might exclaim. And loudly you should! for that phrase is what touches off your recognition of that which we, in our closeness to the actual situation, recognized without need of cue or urge: we were out of doors, out of the doors of our home, on the actual porch, with some cheese, yes, from before, and fruit, yes, but out of doors nevertheless, it was noticed by many of us without cue, and in the cold, and we drank the wine which had been there from before, and some of the leftover bread.

This was not the the worst of it. This was not the worst of the aggravating circumstances, our being stuck vulnerable out on the porch. Our predicament involved also the eventual weariness of the city whose suburb we were. The city was eventually weary of a dearth of excellent music, it turned out, and disagreed with the "sheriff's" actions, at least implicitly. The orchestra was the city's only music, of course, and its only music during our present possession of the symphony orchestra was coming from a back-woods clutch of hoe-clunking rat-jangled hatefuls (as it was related to us by criers, at least, we not needing to go elsewhere, of course, to enjoy some excellent music).

Now it is difficult to relate the actual events which occur in a person's eyes, let alone behind a person's eyes and face, let alone within the minds and spirits of a whole assembly of goodly suburban folk in front of a door containing a symphony orchestra and preventing safety. The Gentle Reader will therefore unfortunately have to accept "Our predicament was so bad that all of us there were gazing fixedly ahead at points representing thoughts, on the walls and air."

It is also unfortunately difficult to represent an angry town and its eventual actions, so said Reader will have to gently accept "Chunks of that music-hungry city came off and headed our way through the streets, chunks even rallied up convoys, suckering thirsty drivers into hauling by truckloads, for good spirits; also, chunks became brutal."

But whatever the events themselves, whatever our gazes, whatever the chunks and their nature, it was the overall indelicacy of the situation (well-whittled little things hurtling through space, angry rights-debating moments, tingles of the atmosphere) that turned our thoughts of the symphony orchestra into a different kind of thought, thought tinged by worry about the negative things that can happen to one, worry about doom, even simple worry about excessive expenditure of effort. And whatever the mechanism, we found that just as our thoughts were darkening thus, our memories of the symphony orchestra—the second fiddles with their screamed poems of objection and despair, the trumpets with their endless stompings—clouded over with a patina of nausea as thick as it was new.

But the orchestra itself was fairly safe and as we died, sending up great greenish gobs of spirit into the ether surrounding our planet, we saw the orchestra poking its guns out of little holes in the masonry and mowing the cityfolk down, and as we mingled together and formed amusing new shapes of many colors in the ether surrounding our planet, we saw the orchestra pick up its instruments and play a nice dirge, perhaps not for us, perhaps not for anyone, but still a dirge, which was appropriate, and as we merged into the streams of history in the ether surrounding our planet we watched the orchestra establish its supermarket and drugstore and also novelty store in which it sold to itself tiny instruments of crafty design, to amuse the new children with while the orchestra was practicing the Mahler, the Bartok, the Mozart, and also that old favorite, Prokofieff.

"Frolic?" Marty said. "Frolic? When the curtains are blanched with tramontane bliss, when freedom sifts dirty through canvas of altars, when peaches remember your hex to parentage—now frolic?"

"Frolic!" said the cheesecake. "Why, frolic! For cattail buttings, palatial esteem-baths, creaturely muck among fab stentorians— frolic! Yes frolic! Today!"

"Oh frolic?" Marty said. "When birds are sack-munched, pad-dished and pus-crippled?"

"Pad-dished? To stand in the way of frolic?"

"To collectivize our euphoria and bounce it off chance like a card in the yesteryear flatulence."

"Oh yeah. Like daisies, remorse, fat bug-eyes, carnivorous witches, palatial goose..."

"Oh. Yeah, like roadtrip serene."

The cheesecake dilemma in the heart of the great Georgia Heritage Wilderness was this: Cheesecake? Not cheesecake?

Marty was fat, enormously fat, poundage bleeding guiltily into the next person's airspace, and cheesecake was not a path for "next sexy," as he called his "lake of attractiveness," as he called his future looks.

But the cheesecake was there in the great Georgia Heritage Wilderness, where the illusion was that air would strip you of untoward bulk, would cleanse your surround including those parts of you constantly mentioned in stories. The air, it was good, and Marty was not so totally fat that he couldn't imagine being stripped of his fat by the air: the good air of the great Georgia Heritage Wilderness, where thinness was a matter of ordinary procedure, so it seemed.

So it seemed! For Marty, having eaten the cheesecake, ending the great Georgia Heritage Wilderness cheesecake dilemma, grew larger and larger, far out of proportion with the three thousand calories now making way through his processes of processing, abutting in even more untoward processes bubbling with stereotypes of gaiety there on his appendia of dessert, dessert and more dessert.

Sad, inhibited Marty!

"Frolic!" Marty said. "For frolic is past and the grip on placebo comes frying the masts of rebellion."

"Frolic?" said the air. "When pertinence gasps, maternity laughs and the chipper gills lap at the slicks?"

"Yes frolic," Marty said. "For when ribbing is limned by apostrophized daredevils, nothing will soothe the unhurt."

"The unhurt? Like you?"

"Like the very mean gods of the trippable underworlds of fashion, like my own sorry craft, like tripartite laughter throughout the various manifestations of excitement."

"You are thinking of religion. That is bad. Perhaps one bite won't hurt you."

Rain in turbid China, back-arching China, ease-kindling China, China adhering, surprised, to thousand-year-old texts. Rain on the fields, into the cracks in Wu-Li's shack. He sits remarking on texts attributable to the vagabond merchant-poets of A.D. 400. His wife is hanging socks on the fireplace. Cheese-crisp Belafonte turns the other cheek to the sufferings of native elderly. He is flying in a greenish plane, plucking courage from his ever-changing situation. This is the China of his grandfather, he is thinking as the engine idles and Belafonte dies with Wu-Li and wife.

Coastal marshes evaporate in California, enticing slat hounds to call in their bundle. "I have a hard time relaxing," John thinks. "Just to let things happen—for that my head is no good. My head is good for terseness, ambition, the turnip endeavor, old chastity, restorement, and vernacular greed—but not for relaxing. Not for letting things happen." He lives in a shack by a road that leads to riches. Carl is churning out miles, engrossed though in shrubs, and the two achieve minutes of horror and John's project loses its impact.

In Bangladesh, a city of coal-black tenements speaking against the sunset idle words of kinship and glory, speaking these words to Martin, who paints, a man is upsetting sausage in cartfuls with horrible veerings. Finally he and Martin, who has a sense of society, lunge at torsi and fall in a hole. The bottom is scattered with broken pots and is lower than Bangladeshi streets.

"A perfect performance," says Robert. "Never a better sweep or swoop of baton. Never a lesser groaning boredom than this I have felt today." Marc Antony, stuck on a passage of Heidegger, yells out his anger. Later Robert loses his cool and the building caves in. Ugly Tuck, picking through horror, finds some beautiful things.

SHADY I BLUSH BUT THE MYSTERY STANDS

I walk down the street in my shady blue eyeshadow sticking my legs into baby carriages and fending off the requisite mothers with great swats of my eyebrows, which send them reeling into New Hampshire, which houses them for a while and then urges them to explore new possibilities.

In the darkroom I emulate the work of Fritz the Cat, who was known to adhere to the principles of modernism except when exploring the virtues of CIA-sponsored gases—these are the times we normally see him.

The pictures show the mothers sailing, sailing, like vagabond, derelict paratroopers. En route they shuffle their recent decisions, notecard by notecard, establishing in their order an aesthetic compromised only by their refuge in the notions of Giotto.

It is a difficult thing to not emulate Giotto.

The babies tickle my feet, which annoys me.

One notecard: "Thursday I will sort the menage of my recreant bludgeonings. List to the side of dilemma!"

Another: "Bankruptcy fueled the fascists—live with it."

The notecards land in Iowa or sometimes Michigan as the mothers think about other things, including my eyebrows. I have one photograph of a mother thinking about my eyebrows, finger to lip, her own eyebrows furrowed to the roots.

The New Hampshire authorities are fed up with me and write letters one per week, which I stow on the ceiling of my bungalow, eventually burning the lot with a gilded candle on a silver candlestick. Several of my neighbors have hurled their fists through the dividers in order to peek. Flames, flames, upward through the roof, into the sky, throwing the soot of New Hampshire authorities letters in an arc whose less than explosive endpoint is often myself, preparing to fling a disgruntled mother into New Hampshire.

Note the disparity: while New Hampshire is urging the previous mother to explore new possibilities, all the while clothing her in the best manner likely, it sends me a letter of the following sort:

You are cordoning vast cataracts of the torrential
blossom of the human maelstrom from the gaze of the
mother-on-the-street with her condolence carriage,
ambling, ambling God only knows where but

*somewhere, and you with your flings. You with your
brows!*

Two things to note: the highly-wrought figures of speech and the
lovely error of calling the carriage "condolence." Is it condolence
walking? It is. The baby cannot walk; the baby is plump and nosy,
a dim hoard indeed; the carriage is, on the other hand, as fine a
stand-in as any for some of the things that some mothers lack,
which leads them to pump themselves up and live with the error.

Perhaps there will come a time when the authorities of New
Hampshire will stop their endless inquests and paste their
25-pound 50% cotton flammable bond to their own ceilings
and see their own neighbors hurl their fists through dividers.
Perhaps that will happen, and then I will throw a modest
celebration in the bathroom of my new home, which will be
likened to Camelot in all the popular journals.

We skinned the elder for refusing, which was true, and for fleeing, which was trumped in the face of the enemy, who swore vengeance should we skin a sitting goat—which is to say, the elder. Many a time! oh, many! had we skinned the fleeing wrong, the warlock aroused and stumbling wildly along our porcupine streets to the imagined safety of his mother's breast, his mother's breast in Anatolia... many a time! So that now, skinning no fleeing duck but rather an angry goat, we felt vindicated, in our feelings of vindication, by the momentum of our righteous skinnings, which had been so many.

But subtleties to theology, to the heavy among us who list to the side of ultimacy. It was all very simple, really, our skinning of this elder, this elder for refusing, and it followed our wrath:

Our wrath at the burial! One mumkins had been buried, one gentle Inanna, one mother of three saintly cubs—but buried, and this is the rub, too soon. For claw her way out she did, up out of the ground on that third day of the year, on that damned day of this world. And out of the grave, her vengeance was vast: vast upon the innocent. Enough of details:

We skinned the refusing elder. He refused our pleas, he refused our warnings of the obvious, which was that Inanna was loose, that mumkins was riveted by thoughts of vengeance. Oh, she was! For eighty of useful ties did she claw, full thirty of certain lineage she devoured, and ten of godly descent she did powder—to the silence of tears. For no one could speak, the questions were so subtle, of such doubtful quality even, so hazy were our ideas about this, so absent the precedents. A rampage, a mother, a mother on a rampage: too soon!

We skinned the elder for his silence, which was no silence of the noble in pain and confusion, no nonplussed oarsman was he. His was the silence of petty immuring, knuckleheaded flight from the chargingly clear; and soon did he learn that we, the nobly indignant, were in our hunching, in our fury, the appanage of one elder's evil; and that we, in our fury, were vents for a cosmic fury too large to behold but in death; and that we were the waves of death.

So far.

"There is no false gospel," he said. "But there is a wrong way to be," he said. "And that way is the way of hesitancy, of not trusting one's instincts but plunging instead into ways at best insincere, at worst disastrous, as, I am sorry to say, I judge this presentation of anger to be." That was not the worst of it.

"I say." He died, suffering none too much for the ineptitude of his quarrels, alone among his oarsmen. His dainty oarsmen, owing much, paid little but this elder's skin to Inanna.

But that, we know, was quite enough.

The Havana Diary

11/29/86
(development, death of what happened, Monks' House, Shropshire)

The verdure was terrific. That was the first thing, massive embryo knots and scallywag rhizomes, the foliage, the dew with its glints. Cathy looked and her eyes were a party of schoolmarms gone public in their unchastity. I resented her, I resented this forest. I resented the stature of the Philippine Revolution as it artificially snagged in the birch. As it snagged a man leaned out and proclaimed my Cathy to me from a scroll that reached to the ground. "Hasty assumptions she never destroys! Your misgivings do reach their object! The people are aware of her power!" I hated this man who was? yes—simpering in false majesty of engineered accidence. I engorged myself with my hate and empowered it, allowed it to grab a stick and take a swipe that missed by inches; the Revolution moved up a branch. I asked Cathy if I could use her shoulders a moment. "You're losing perspective, darling. This is a *revolution*." I clacked my teeth as the Revolution turned on its camera lights. "The Revolution of facts! This is the Philippine Revolution! In this, the forest. The forest for our amusement. The forest for love." Cathy was entranced and the man in the Revolution waved to her in between outbursts of propaganda. I grabbed her arm and—burst! it was solid. It was hard. Burst! I was tired. My legs were bending all over. I was growing perceptibly softer. I felt I might suddenly spread, ooze, cream out my insides right up to the beckoning embouchure of the next metropolis. The man in the air was getting tired, too, as he proclaimed ever more succinctly the virtues of my rock-hard Cathy, his Revolution, their forest. I noticed then that Cathy was glowing, at first faintly around the edges, then brilliantly all over. The point of radiation seemed to move within her, and she expanded each part to englobe it. She was huge, her eyes now headmistresses in ointment, and I nailed the force of my assumptions to the birch until it fell, with a dismal, fluid plop, to the soft, sparkling-clean surface of this euphoric computer of purchase we were calling the forest.

9/30/56
An early birthday surrounded by relatives! Tried to extract my

mambo from their interp, found a certain *reason* lacking, intelligent *grasp*, mature *fluidity*. Closed in on the least of them, extracted forthwith rum, coins, a sense of the ideal. (Flogged himself after.) (Found dead in a cabinet. Teeth?) (Interesting because he'd been noticing my teeth.) "Teeth!"
Extraction?

7/12/89
There is a wolf and it is partying in my pants. It is raising its great wolfy head and, full with the brine of apocalypse, is roaring inside-out about latex and the smooth bends of its own complexion, the same toilet complexion of Born-Again Jesus and patty-cake in the staterooms of Kansas. It is alone in a room, this wolf-pants combo, and really it's static, there are blobs, occasional blobs, little bubblings too, rivulets of this or that going prrrrrroot! prrrrrrroot! down the hideous toilet complexion—the wolf is a mighty he—in this room—this eerie room, a room with sadness to it. "This is where they make the mighty 3Z17," the snazzy young guide told us. "This room is sure to go down in..." The 3Z17, it turns out, remains void of description, a secret engine, disaster-causer perhaps, perhaps grief-bringer to the multitudes, not to be known by any save the grown in the art of populace.
Wait, maybe I'm wrong. My pants are moving. The wolf in my pants has noticed 3Z17 and is sort of bubbling under the skin, a cute, gentle bubbling of nothing at all, and then it's suddenly haranguing the spectators, adult, in the way of the large-nosed De Gaulle, Updike, ethnics. He is at first quite fluent and then as the notions get tricky it's "sumuuurrrrrfff, sumuuurrrrrfff, sumuuurrrrrfff," and closet Bo does the correct thing, kitchen Rich does the correct thing, they all assume their variegated poses with one intent in mind: extraction.
Extraction?

12/1/67?
Invalid:
Producing extreme, distracting contractions of the *glottus mediagolmis*. Am finding it hard to concentrate on the matters at hand, the matters at hand, which the shining jewel of careening benevolence Adolf Braunschweiger says are the matters at hand, the matters at hand. This is hard because the switch, the radio,

certain wavelengths of radiation all speak to me, endeavor on my bands with their manifold attractions, derelictions, propriety. Causing contractions. Consider the chessboard: a slogan arises. "Che's bored of revolution! Only pawns!" But more, more in the media, more than any slimy matrix of desires ever bargained for: cheese on Sunday, curtains in the Palace of Sausage, polysorbate-60. And the revolution plays itself out in Adolf, assuming greater tones as we lapse in our daily attention, lapse lapse lapse.... Larger, larger: the new army planes flown by those who have "swooned," who have "spiralled" into the utmost sphere of correct endeavor, the matter at hand, who are charming at it, who glint from the edges of our perception in their absolute perfection of attachment, attachment, these new planes, carrying no passengers, certainly none who have denied the absolute centeredness of the matter at hand in their actions, tones, affections, common-sense reactions to loss and development, these new planes have only two wheels on the wings, the rear having been removed in favor of a fuel tank, one in the front as well.... A ticket is hard to get but if you get one it's the matter at hand and they take off and when you all agree you land and then the only way to keep from blowing up is to keep going quite fast with ailerons 37 degrees or so all the length of the runway and then some quite far and fast until the fuel is all used up and then we need something new to think about. Departures on the minute. Why don't you take these planes and consider the similar things with rabbits, endives, roots, the cringing in the wings, adrenalin infusions, trucks.... I mean I'm living a life, the matter at hand suggests itself to me, and I'm living a life, want to live a decent life, enjoy the matter at hand with its manifold joys and the matter of contractions confronts me and I descend! Down pits of hell. Amen. Amen. It's gone.

3/18/01.
Overheard at the Chung Bible Emporium:

> Angora kitty, speak attractive
> slogans like "meal, meal" or
> "holy as the fragments of his decency's chasuble"
> for me in my restaurant
> I own a restaurant
> and stagger I don't care if you stagger stagger

to hell for all I care stagger out
the true remnants of my glory past for me in my restaurant
I am a discotheque

9/9/89
The Architects.
Oh it is odd indeed that the men in charge have trumped the
charges against these entrepeneurs and denied them all access to
deep history. When in fact it is in the nature of the thing, we living
in those, that has fettered their endeavor. That has rent their
desires, scattered their would-be emolument, fragmented the nations of their teeming rises. No, nothing. Nothing at all. Can save
the builders of our scapes

Hysterical Margaret, languid only on my flaccid breast, speak loud your troubles to this uncle. Hello?

"Oh uncle, when Robbie did secure his boasts by all his friends, and then there was no taste of you, I throbbed, and clubbed my holies there, and looked washed out for lack of gilt statements of the honest, homey truth. So that now I need a density of love, a dosage wild for my honey cheeks, lest suddenly I all unleash."

Oh have no fear, sweet Margaret, you hysterical, do not undo your girth for mere unstabling of a captured die. My love is dense as dense can be, my love is wrought so heavy on my grizzled brow, my love is hard and wayward. I give you endless monolithic statements of your golden flights, your drizzling temper, the fierceness of your being in its case. Hello?

"Oh uncle, this evening have I food consumed, a barrelful and more."

Don't worry. Eating is a master's joy. You, master of the in and out. When I grow beat I shall not eat, but you are well, and you must swell.

"Extra loathing upon you, uncle." She crashes out of the house and calls in through a window: "A major stampede of ill determination upon you, uncle."

"My favorite aunt! If you knew my travails...."

"The work and shove of the young? The efforts unending to start a new way?"

"*Au contraire.* It is not so funny with us, my aunt. We, though small, have serious concerns. Death and affliction of limb are not unknown to us, nor strange, nor even unusual, ever. Scents bear more than one message. Sights are the rowdiest cousins of pain. Aunt, you mustn't make mock of our dusk."

"Dusk? Dusk you invoke?"

"Dusk the beseecher. Dusk the screaming beseecher to follow, to death."

"My child, the work of adult is most sultry."

"Not worse than the work of small child."

"Dusk is the time when adult gazes weeping over fields usurped and abandoned, pledges to keep out of trouble in future, but knows that all time is a ribbon. To start a new way is impossible now; we must repose in pleasure."

"We have only change: change the unbearable death every second, change that corrupts the last minute's light, stupid, stupid change. How could you envy the maelstrom child? unholy whirlwind kid?"

"And dusk? Such melancholy in a time of day?"

"Your melancholy would be joy for us. Dusk for us is new deaths giving birth to deaths unimaginable, which will swoop and tempt and finally eat in the morning. So at night, to forestall deaths' eat, we like our rooms cheerful; pillows cost money, curtains cost money, all the soft things and fun, mean toys cost money, but money is only one death, one death at the seat of our nights' survivability, which we accept. Money is easy for us to accept, that is one problem we do not have."

"Would you like to go to the Superbowl?"

"The Superbowl I do not like, my aunt, my favorite aunt. But chocolate is good!"

Greg is fairly matchless, I found out today. The reasons for this, which I am expatiating on for the *Journal of Bereavement Psychology*, are numerous: upbringing, compromise with the inevitable, genes (belonging to many distinct, but collusive in matters of taste, branches of the Indo-European and Sinitic gene families).

Over lunch, it turns out, he admonished me on some habits I had been ignoring. I have a good many, and Greg is an avid spotter of behavioral anomalies. While I do not usually care to attune myself to the damage I do my environment, Greg's eye excepts its marks from havering to the degree that many of them, indeed thousands (Greg's eye is as large as our habitat), have thrummed headlong into subtler chords, without all-trouncing guilt.

I explained my methods and feelings. It was through my rather sharp education I could enter and exit a good many paths towards virtue and other extremes without ever being in danger of donning the ancestral tunic or shrugging off the precipitate blowtorch of our well-staffed sanctity.

But Greg was there.

There were also a fair dozen redheads caroming off the highway under which we were lunching in that type of day-of-the-dreadnought newfangled luncheon spot so plaguing of the creatures who would angle us sharper. One of the caroming cluster bent his young head over the lip of the highway and spoke of the Gauls, those infamous shunners, and spoke of our being like Gauls (Greg, it turned out, had noticed the thing a good month before), and it was razor-sharp on the palate, his notion, his sense of our place, and Greg looked off into space, which for you and me is like dying of bad contraception in the eighteenth month, so of course I was shocked, and spoke heavily to the redhead, who threw his reddish young body over the lip in a lithe young red stunt, holding on to the lip with his lithe young red hands, and facing me backwards, he turned his head to control my anxiety but only that he might with his odd reddish limbs envelop me backwards, this redhead now hanging in air, and this quieted Greg down some and he seemed to get an idea concerning my habits, which I had been ignoring until this quite lucky lunch.

"You know," he said as the redhead clung tighter and entered some special new parts in the fray, "I think you, like most of the people I've known, have been ignoring some vital facts about yourself, and spend much of your trouble (for trouble is work, undertaken most often in earnest) divesting yourself of the obvious, facts like 'gunning to Jakarta I could not help seeing the flames of Mylanta factories nudging the peers of Roland into halftones,' or like 'gluing my headdress to want is a difficult and unchampioned but so-vital work in the age of utterly gunless accoutrements.'"

There was more, but the upshot of the whole beast was a sullen, matte stand against undue violence. "Terrific," one says, "and then we will scream for a while."

Criticism

The ballocks of Mort were dropped from an altitude of three miles directly over Denver, the highest city already, so you can imagine. They fell through wafts and whips of the air to a spot behind Gruesome Hilarity, a patch of lively merchants devoted to importing substances of the widest possible appeal to the citizenry of Denver. As Gruesome Hilarity nodded and minced, displaying many of those habits known to derive from untrammeled pursuit of that which is rightfully latched upon by a mass known as audience, the ballocks of Mort descended into a smaller patch of lavender growing with vegetal aplomb behind Gruesome Hilarity's northmost member, Buford. Only he noticed them, and returning the questioning glance of Becky, questioning because Buford was swathed head to toe in ballock-fill, Buford dismissed the errantry of Mort's parts with shrugs and flicks of the brightest effectiveness, the tautest charm, the gleefullest tongue, and agents of the Museum for Life Happenings marched into him and began snapping off parts of his body, encasing them one by one in the museum's traditional vestiture, velveteen bordered with gentian sea-flesh, gentian-inked sponge, for instance. This was, they explained, because parts of Mort do not often fall from the sky from an altitude of three miles directly into Gruesome Hilarity or anywhere near it, and the fact that this happened and, moreover, Buford was there to receive it with disingenuous greeting, was proof of a link between the work of Baldessari and Christo...

Bun-kick one, bun-kick two. Everyone is bun-kicking with the exception of Charles, who wafts around like a tick on a twenty-year habit. He is reading a book about sodomy and getting fat on cheeses like explorateur cheese and having some bankruptcy proceedings always on hand in case he should need them.

Everyone besides Charles, bun-kick and bun-kick. This is for the tension of buttocks, tense with muscle of the buttocks. Charles's buttocks are soft as the sorrow on good Anne Boleyn being carted out by the henchmen of her husband's enemies. Charles's chest is full of its nipples, his stomach a gas-stop for laughter. Charles himself is so constructed as to make you think certain things, for a very long time, if you examine him closely. Few ever do.

Charles is terrible with finances as he watches the others do bun-kick, bun-kick. His memory of a point of law is not forthcoming, there as he watches the bun-kicks. The bun-kicks make him think of his cousin Ham, who died of construction work. That was a tragedy for the family and its friends, the other family. It was enough to drive young Charles right out of the family seat and into the world of finance. Now, bad finance.

Charles is unlikely to participate in the bun-kick thing going on. He finds it reminds him of a dead cousin, and if it didn't he might find it revolting.

Several of the bun-kickers now sit down and pray. They are praying to their god, the god of dipping-into-confusion-without-being-swallowed. With him they hope to emerge very huge very soon. If all works out they will swing with the hottest, manage with greats and parade the whole width of them seriously, seriously, down streets known for the total cohesion of audience.

Charles has been known to encourage prayer, and now as there's prayer going down he feels somewhat happy. He looks at everyone praying and there's a feeling in him of being on solid ground, in a solid country, with solid ideas about a great number of things. He grows afraid that this is all illusion. The class lets out, and he watches each woman and man step out into daylight in fewer steps than previously. He thinks.

How I Discovered Many Things and Became Well-Known for Helping the Infirm in Moments of Explosion

I was the sort of melancholic whose greatest joy was in glamorizing the effete. Give me an effete, I would say, I'll show you one tremendous effete. There is nothing like an effete, I would say, the mother-of-tenebrous type who surrounds himself with the gangly in order to swat at delusions, predominant now as always among the gangly because of their stretch, which while metric can have its way in the dunk-and-slit fractional mind of man, always thirsty, man not mind, for facts. The effete, taking to task the gangly for hearty delusions: nothing at all like him. Give me just such an effete, or any.

The effete: utter man. I soon found myself in contact with vast stretches of the effete lining several highways, those big bright roads you cross through cornfields and some of the very best scenery anywhere. Few notice them, but they notice you, and are saddened. Their sadness extends into most of their work and ways of considering truths, and it is in fact seldom that those particular effete by the highway can accept the teachings of their native church. Too dramatic, the teachings, and not dramatic enough. Too concerned with riddling the formidable with the unintelligible, or vice versa. Both full of holes, offending effete.

Taut, heavy effete! I found very few of them in the best-dressed places, the centers of cities, where everyone was on the way to a formal discussion of flauntings. In those places, people's effeteness leanings were stymied, fingered by humdinger jiggers of this or that brew, disaster brew usually, utterly uninspiring, and effeteness could never withstand such robotic.

The rich ones I found in museums, to no one's surprise. My friends were expecting something like that, museums full of effete, and told me so. I had listened and placed an acne-scarred chin on hands and dishevelled said chin and prepared an itinerary of which I adhered to a simplified version, and a table of likelihoods and habits, and a gloss of catchphrases often preferred by the ones who show up in museums (according to friends), and was ready in all sorts of ways long before the event of my going.

Then, of course, there was the matter of contacting many government agencies, bureaus of this or that, and private companies large and small whose dealings with the effete were legion. Of these there were ten.

My pay was usually hourly, few knowing the thread of public opinion or what beat it warps through semantics. Covenants, each in a different mind, wafting or wilting according to stench of the stand-up, prop-up, or stuck, every aspect a different source of the grue-world odor, my job to test and prod until each mind's covenant might consider in one clause or other my client's item, effete, and said item's effeteness, and so on.

Many people said many things to me then and after, things of cunning and amber, slitting my somber hang of it lively, and then I grew rich and had no need to prod the zaftig as did most of my sad, curb-dwelling friends with their cunning facts on museums.

THE DIFFICULTY THERE WAS IN PLEASING OURSELVES

"Much immersion was going down in this part of the environment; many of us were getting some hands-on experience that we hadn't bargained for, living somewhat dazed in the circumference of our blandness, giving everything for the mania to come, listing in our habits like beehive trawlers in milk, owning up to the closets and windmills and sitcoms," the TV says.

I don't understand the difference between a windmill and a sitcom. Mary says they are similar in that both are convivial. Both are convivial, she goes on, in circumstances like those in which you find yourself retching uncontrollably after the garbageman declares himself homeless. In such a situation, difficult as it may be for you, a windmill can seem quite convivial. Same with a sitcom.

Different—a different matter, Mary says, wise. The sitcom seen on the days the windmill is not seen is different there, because of that—days.

I agree with Mary on everything, though I disagree with most things in general. I agree with Mary's assessment of standard commodities and their likelihood of continuance. She is determined to believe they will continue; I am sure they will too. It is unusual for us to believe in other things that people usually believe in, such as aging. And yet we believe in those things that many believe in, such as continuance of commodity. How do we do it? Should we be doing it?

I leaf through the mad attractions in the weekend paper. Who is this playing at the farmhouse? How is his band built? When do we get to understand his many motivations, no matter how painful? When are we finally permitted to disown those fat slobs who pain us too much, who insist on their bulk, who insist *we* insist on their bulk, who are fat, fat brats? When?

Is this the proper venue for the band that is mentioned? Is this where we run around screaming at the days that have passed too quickly, in sing-song? Do we *join* the band? Do we *repudiate* it? Do we seem to march too quickly, or do we march too softly? Is this afternoon or is this evening? When does it seem that the most things happen?

More questions raised by the bulk of this story: How large a canvas must Miró have to develop his life into something more sordid? Is it okay to want Miró's life more sordid, or would that imply a different history, a no-no for our thinkings? Are we raised in the barn only to shoot the canary? Do we graft our battalions stark, stark onto others' battalions, or lift the embargo chord by chord?

Are we to remodel the albatross? Bankrupt the staid? Bankroll the stale? Are we to massage the elders, or are we to be massaged by them? Massage them, be massaged by them? Are we to admire boys who dance well? Are we to admire well-dancing boys? Is it often that we are allowed to be as dull as it is our intention to be? Is the answer to that "No one can tell"?

Am I a gooseneck lamp? Have I stuttered once too often?

If I read the palm of the greatest tennis star on earth, will I grow up to malign imbroglios involving lack of tennis ball, or such? Will I not?

How We Met

What a wonderful, beautiful, excellent machine, the balloon!

—Gondolfier

At first it was cruel, it was truly cruel shoes. We went about as if in a daze, as if the whole world were a fuzzy bowl. Were we, in fact, in a daze? It seems unlikely. But the result was the same, and it was cruel.

Bump! we went, bump! People, disconcerted by the collisions, would give the cold shoulder, regardless of any other factors. Dogs, yelping, would speed away into the night, supposing us to be vampires or bandits or cruel robbers. And we, alone, would stand unawares, hearing many sounds, understanding nothing.

That, then, was how we met Rodolf Gondolfier, a balloonist. On the first night before the spring equinox, just when things start getting happy in the households, the man, seeing our state, came up and gave us each in turn a live child to care for. Assuming, it would seem, that a sense of importance would be born of the responsibility. In this he was typical, so far: in the belief that we lacked a sense of importance. Very well, a fuzziness existed, we were out of *the* realms, but were we out of *all* realms? Was it truly the end, this blocking-out of our palaver from the streams of Man? Assumptions made, admittedly, hastily. Yet who can forgive the insensitivity of the healthy?

Back to Gondolfier. This man, despite his careless assumption, was unique in the effusiveness of his manner. Live children were contraband at the time; a certain danger lurked in the air. But bring he did, and before we knew it, why there were a good passel of runts assembled before our bodies. We named them, though they already had names: this was to instill a true sense of proprietorship. We named them Candy and Joel and Rubicon and Flo and Cherished and Sidney and Frangie and Pretzie. At the end of the naming, which took place on a roof, we had cookies and fruit, and some of us offered some to the children in the first gestures of protection— this although no formal introduction to the art of puericulture had yet been given us by this man, Rodolf Gondolfier. That he intended to show us the ropes was evident, but as yet he was silent.

The truth of the matter is this: he was, in a limited respect, irresponsible. He did not live up to this promise of instruction, he did not even mention it again during his entire benefit stay. Which meant that it was all up to us. Now do you know what? Have you been paying attention? If so, you will have noticed that some of us had already started on our parenting there on the roof. Well, those few were in advance of the rest of us. Head start. There was nothing to be done, we sprinted out from the void we were in and accomplished things ourselves as well: a fruit here, a chuck roast here, everything was soon in order.

Frangie died. He was the first. Someone noticed that we had named him after the adjective "frangible" and said that perhaps this was the cause of his demise; the rest of us pooh-poohed the suggestion. He died, we thought, from a lack of vegetables: vegetables, it was obvious, were lacking in sufficient quantity to supply necessary vitamins and minerals. We purchased vegetables. With the chucks and the fruits and now the vegetables, we could count on healthy and immortal (from our point of view) kids.

It wasn't interesting, however. Rubicon, fourteen, would often amuse us with his parlor tricks, with his handstands and footswings and headflips, but he was the only skilled among them. And of his tricks we soon tired. They paled, his tricks. So we ordered new ones. And when he told us in that mincing voice of his that he knew no more but that he could (and here we detected a wink) find some at the library, we suspected infidelity and a wish to go forth into the world. But was he not a gift? He didn't know our force. We attached our Rubicon to the statue of Goliath hard by the refectory, Goliath with pan flutes, and left him overnight. In the morning he was gone, abducted. It was normal, we said, and we were disconsolate a good long time, so we cared extra joyously for the rest.

But they can do little. One little girl can read, and she reads us stories; one little boy can swim, and he splashes us with water when we need to be clean; one child has a horse-laugh that can furnish joy at times.

But in truth we are chopfallen. Our slough of despond cannot be masked, our gloom is not contrivance. We are alone, these children tell us, we are alone alone alone. Gondolfier is cruel, he is truly cruel shoes.

THERE WAS A FAIR HUNK OF NICENESS OFFERED US THERE:
THE FIVE-YEAR-OLD'S GUIDE TO GROWING UP STRAIGHT
Propaganda

There was the day I left and headed out to the aerodrome where a great machine was awaiting me, and I entered it and considered myself one with the mass of beings therein who saluted me with one hand.

It was a long time before I could get to the rear of the thing and salute, there, the gigantic "standing officer," who was three times the height of the thing and engorged on confetti, which rained over the other occupants of the thing as he hiccoughed for minutes which seemed like years—were in fact years, that's why he "stood on us"—and the occupants hated him somewhat but certainly not a lot, and I loved him with much of my heart.

"Hello," I said. I expressed a good many things I haven't expressed to anyone else. I broke down and wept, in fact, and brought my wife and child into the picture—holding the wife by my pinky, the child by the ring in my septum—and described a lot of events that encircled not only myself and this requisite wife and this requisite child but also the life of the whole community (because of extension). I was molar-decrepit! femur-rejected! bladder-tumescent! lemur-senescent! Lemur, lemur, shoved up with flaws. Many of those broad sorrows descendant on lapdogs of the most civilized peoples arrayed themselves against me like one arrow, two arrow, three, and I stood brave as chiggers, as slapstick besotted the clues by which I, or we, might escape this beaming flap.

He, of course, didn't speak.

Then I calmed down and everything was okay and I launched into a sack of my orneriness using the full complement of elves crouched beneath the feet of the people now behind me (geometry flails and swoons)—the elves rising up and describing in one breath the massing of loaves at the gentrification of wheezes, a prime elf holiday. My orneriness did not last.

Everything scurried about!

"Banish me to the hum and the drum of solicitousness," someone said. I turned to him and with nebulous eye told of shrieking and limping and sodden frenzies this way and that way, all.

"Yes," he said, quite grateful.

The machine lifted off and described its familiar curlicue through the matchless streets of heaven, cloud after cloud quite uncontrary. The pilot was somewhere boarded up and hungry, taught *not* to expect much from those masses who will respect you up the yin-yang because you are a pilot, lieutenant. The rest of us shimmied around our capsules of sluggishness and perfection like so much dimness in a cabriolet.

OUR LIFE IN MUD

We sprinted around the muddy enclosure for two hours until one of us started falling down; the other leaned over to help him up and the downed one yanked hard on the arm of the helper, toppling him. The mud was cool and unforgiving.

We found this new posture congenial until some postcards were made by the haberdashery journal for distribution to haberdashers up and down the coast that they might give them to respectful clients who purchase enough; in the postcards were us, in the upper left corner, our names variously scripted in the upper right, our mothers' and fathers' likenesses etched as if by a three-year-old in the lower right, and a real bomb (like a letter bomb but smaller and even simpler) in the lower left.

We got up and intercepted the postcards, smearing them with mud but preventing their woeful arrival in merchant hands. We spoke on the radio: something was wrong with our nation that such as explosives could wend their way doomingly to the merchants of finery.

Meanwhile, the people who had imprisoned us in the muddy enclosure became angry and demonstrated with fists and legs against our continued position of having escaped. They moved their fists up, down like pistons chomping on rabid mollusks; their legs were gridiron taffy, imprisoning versatility of mien and development. The commentators spoke long about this; had our preventing of bombs to the haberdashers warranted present position of life in the globe of all waftings, our encampment in sturdiness railing?

We had our own plan. We readdressed the postcards to greengrocers instead, and sent them—hoping to show city hall the valor of men who would keep such things from happening, men who would lift themselves whole up out of muck and into a face of saving.

The greengrocers blew up one by one, recalling each a verse of Kipling and screaming it till the end of breath through the larynx. This horrified the multitudes, who bought stopwatches and counted the hundredths since death of the last greengrocer.

The stopwatch gentry surrounded us with tokens of gladness but we refused, citing our service to law and dire need on the part of citizenries at home and abroad.

Finally we got tired of the whole mess and went back to our muddy enclosure and raced around, racing around and around, till one of us started to fall and the other, gallant, reached down, only to fall into congeniality with the first in a gradual approximation of homosexual ecstasy in which one partner, screaming for some reason or other, finds a love for the other deep in his throat that can only be said with vulgar actions.

Later, tremendous improvement.

EVENT OF A BOY WHO THINKS TOO MUCH

I am breakfasting. This is the scene I've looked forward to for well over half the night, and over it is a scroll, and on each side of the scroll a tiny and, when examined with an electron microscope, exquisitely beautiful boy. The scroll says, simply, "BREAKFAST," and the food I am eating is various, ridged, involved in itself and tremendous.

I walk out into the Everglades which surround my house and examine them. There are fifteen miles in one direction and fifteen miles in another, each replete with the latest in exquisite dilemmas of beauty. I run my foot along the mud of the nearest area and find it as soft as the skin of my favorite sex partner, Bruno.

The sun is high in the sky by the time I withdraw my foot from the mud. I look at the sun and peel part of my back away to expose what looks to my angry, confused eyes to be Stalin. Stalin yelling at troops, unlawful things full of brutality, the murder of millions. However, he opposed Hitler and that fills me with a certain respect that cannot bridge, however, the gulf between my attraction to my normal back and the repugnance I feel towards this one, which, juncture notwithstanding, I somehow can't feel as my own.

There is evil in the air today, I think to myself, forgetting my flapping back, waving my hair in the wind which soon picks up to such a point that it brings me and my open Stalin up over some rooftops which are quite far from my hovel amid the Everglades and then on through the unattractive realms of the monkeyers, the fragmentary stalwart, the hideous-kidneyed betrayers of soot, the latchkey celebs. Soon I am over New York, which looks especially shiny in this strange air which, I repeat, is evil today, and there is such smell about that I wonder who made things, the world and all its effects and celebs and beauty queens, and I fall into pieces and three of them go right through Angus the Frontiersman, making him do an odd medieval ballet on the pavement to death, and three of them go through Zvi, who is lounging about in his underwear wishing there was something more to this gaudy, fat sun in the sky than balls and balls of sheer precociousness—how difficult, after all, a sun filled with gaunt vitality when it is slick with the grease of its exhumations: the biggest dilemma of all.

That is all, and the story ends. I am nothing, but soon a familiar thought comes to fix me: "I live mostly in the realm of the imagination." I pulse a bit and grow into something quite clumsy: an unordered truth, unwanted, unfinished....

I think it's true of most people, they live in imagination almost only. Some maybe not. Maybe some people live every day in a real way without imagination. They see the TV and when they see it see some colors or not, some guys or girls in colors or not, some movement and buildings and fire and so on. They go outside and see some men and women walking around or sitting still and feeding the pigeons and maybe they know what the pigeon-feeders are thinking and feeling because how many things can you feel when you're feeding some pigeons. Those people don't add to what we see so they're invisible. I think that's true of most people, they're invisible, so maybe in fact most people—we could call them "trash" with unfortunate accuracy—don't see what's imaginative but only what's real, and they just walk around repelling everyone 'cause it's obvious they don't add to the commonweal: repellent.

Myself, when I exit imagination and enter the real and live in it as if it were my birthright, which it is, I get incredibly moved and also scared, and I have to leave pretty much right away, though it's hard to leave that fast and the effort's so great I try to remember, I program myself in odd ways that themselves contribute to the imaginative slick of my life, to stay away from the real and just work, work, work the way I'm able and used to, which is with an abject contemplation based on being spared from reality, originating in that gratefulness.

Now I have rescued myself from a freakish but nice obliteration by means of my funny self-evident spurt of philosophy which means nothing at all but its fact. My life will continue in a freakish and often not-nice way, and things will start in, and breakfasts will soon be glorious in the Everglades once again.

I Was a Passive-Aggressive Homeowner Type

> The house when ugly
> devises serenity
> shod in gaffes to
> uphold the pillars
>
> —Medieval Italian foundation-
> stone inscription

In the 'fifties, a lot of things would go down that couldn't be categorized. This was in the era of my father's relative youth, when he would drop by the local sanitation union and demand higher wages, for the conversation. This was when Judy Garland was refreshing herself with Italians, underscoring everyone's urge to know Italian. This was a time of radical decisions, urgent news, and the flare-ups of hostility we have come to categorize with almost alarming perspicuity.

The 'fifties were a time for many men to examine themselves. A lot of examination went down then, a lot of interesting knowledge came shuffling out of the necks and chests of men, a lot of wives grew dusky wearing their best for a possible chat with the man who, we know now, was engaged in definitions of the Other that only such as we can unravel. These definitions clustered around the great moments of our enlightenment and strangled them or helped haul them up into the bad air of the shipyards: the *Cleopatra*, apparently, had a disgusting prow.

How, how, how could the moments of our enlightenment, caught by definitions snaking out of the necks and chests of men, survive the apparently awful butt of the *Cleopatra's* prow? Is the *Cleopatra* to indict, or are the definitions snaking out of the necks and chests of men and hauling up the moments of our enlighten-ment, during an era whose wives grew dusky thinking about their men and the possible conversations with these huggers of the synopses, blasters through the wherewithal of negative combines, stumblers foot by foot through the matchless disgrace of existence to the chair of their wives' melancholia?

Are we to blame the men, the definitions, or the *Cleopatra*? If we do all three, are we not asking for a profusion of recoil? If we indict one and only one, are we not asking for the failure, with possible catastrophe, of yet another system the source of whose confidence, by spring or recoil, must be seen as the definitions so dastardly changing the moments of our enlightenment by their hauling into the lusty air of the shipyard?

May we blame nothing, sleep with the awesome correctness of each moment's redaction, live for the scrupulous as we reject all scruples, and have lives of pure scruple as the scrupulous fades? Is this allowed?

Are we?

Irrelevant! This is a story of the 'fifties, when I was zero to four, already in possession of my parents' houses, which numbered eight. I was betrayed by three nursemaids. In the morning I would refresh myself with the bloom of the canvas, my elder brother being a sculptor who painted his sculptures, as so many did. I laughed it up with the corner grocer, the pathetic young barmen of my father's enterprise, the nursemaids who failed me. I called for pistachios—pistachios were brought. I ate through the safety of blinding, I lip-synched to buffalo. In every way my life resembled that of a monster.

Except in one. Still, there are many questions. And was it really one? Only one? As many as one? Will I return? Will we?

HE-MAN MOMENTS:

THE MATCHLESS SHAFTS OF EVENTFULNESS

There will be no morale problems in the
First Marine Expeditionary Force because
I say there will be morale. There also will
be no boredom.

> —General Alfred Gray addressing
> troops in the Persian Gulf during
> the war

After a thousand years the men have
begun to lose energy....

> —*The Faggots and their Friends be-
> tween Revolutions*, Larry Mitchell,
> p. 51

I am a big macho shithead.

> —David "Missy" Mueller

I IMPROVE YOUR CONFIDENCE IN ORDER TO FUCK YOU
JOYOUSLY FOR US BOTH

"I am sweet, o young, mod dancer."

"You? *I* fret the stars—chanting, mating the stomach's mix to the feast of several well-known meats, causing the well-enmeshed to refrain from 'mush! mush!' at crude, angry beasts—and the stars, well-fretted by me, enjoy a flashing up the whole-tone scale, down the half-tones-intermixed-with-certain-whole-tones scale well-known by you and me, and finally exhibit the greatest merit to one and all, flaming, choosing the right sort of wildness there in the sky for each reader to spank, euphorically, lapping it up like the stalwart bionics of the '70s and their plaid-shitted poodles, terrific, terrific I say metaphorically as well as with a certain *embryo* in my manner of speech, which speaks well of the factors, those nicely wrought factors so terrific in our environment, the flat-fact environment of the much-described moderns...."

"You speak of the moderns! That is *you*. *You* are the moderns, euphoric, guilty yes but contrived too much to be solely a mess, cheese in your gifts, cheese and no end of cheese in your gifts. I am terribly given to admiration of those sweet cheeses of your gifts, those life-mentioning cheeses so curtly propounded by you, there in your slip-up meringue life of solid, unmitigated silk. But I—and this I must hammer like sad tickles upon your flatulent, ever-flatulent ears—I am sweet, as sweet as the seven 'hithers' of Annabelle the mistaken-for-tiny, as sweet as any journey of breezes mothering qualms upon the sick breast of an autumn day such as, say, this. This day, I mean."

"Your math is clean. Your platitudes reek, however, of seventeen mute and scream-wearied bladder infections—rectitude-burnished though they be, though they be. I, unlike the palsied modern musics...."

"You, perhaps, are not so understanding of that which is called 'your musty, love-maggoty emanations of pore.' Meaning yours, for it is only by you that I repel myself, only by you that my fiery senses five are trapped in a poorly mittened game of 'Here it is the other's clock.' If you knew your own clasping match of lips, your own flight of gas-bedraggled eyelids, your own fusty septum, you would not, as I see you do, berate the myriad gumptions of your obvious frame."

"For I am not nearly so flip and ill-cordoned as that putrid flank, that putrid flank of a colt, a colt so downright unrighted by slack...."

"Modern? Your so-called modern musics?"

"Yes."

"I have only to nod in your direction, in the flat-chit direction of the clammy, pariah-basted monkey-wanna-be that you aren't (I scream your plastic sky-high, I bereave you of no suddenness)—I have only to nod for you to be what you are, the total semblance of everything chosen, the monster of nice conception in the unhappy dais outside the choice vacation spot of several honorable-mention sorts, nice conception like a perfect bumpkin upon that structure, that joyous, elite structure turned sad and shunned suddenly, mysteriously, one summer long ago—but that is a story with Kate."

A police van arrives, police reciting delectable apricot fudge in its full ingredients—"Howdy, Sergeant Major."

"Howdy, vendor. You're blockin' traffic."

"Blockin' my ass, I'm blockin'."

The dust rises cool and fluid dynamic around the wheels of onrushing cars.

"Would you help me kindly, Sergeant Major?"

"The ice cream vendor needs not ask."

"My boys are searching the median environment for some sort of way, they've got string and a certain panache but no real *highly developed* means of reducing traffic flow in the passing direction in favor of stoppage for sweets, and I was wondering if you mightn't favor the ice cream vendor industry with a means and a way of furthering selfsame stoppage, I'm not suggesting mildly, nor suggesting no wild affront, you know..."

The officer looks past the barrelling cars at the ice cream men on the median with their ounces of string and the placards, etc. He takes a look at his men, natty in black with coy tilts to their caps, extravagant men, refusals of various sorts already glowing around their edges, and blows with full police lungs on his whistle. "Take out your guns, snarly metal, take out! And, I say, aim! Fire! Read your rulebooks! Aim! We're in real-life jeopardy, sons, men, we're having no wee appraisal from bums in pancake galoshes, no sir, we're out on the fast-hanging streets, and it's us who're doing the hanging. Take aim! Take fire at will! The vendor's your man."

The ice cream vendor ducks and crawls to his truck amid a volley of .22 bullets. A wheel hisses. Many cars stop. The ice cream vendor, finally, dead, attracts a crowd which rushes at little-publicized flavors, handed out by the vendor's men, now by the truck, congratulating where congratulations are due, and slowly the sun sinks behind the hills to a rousing hurrah! ahoy! hoohooey!

Later, at the morgue, the ice cream vendor's mother removes a silk scarf from her son's reddened pocket and places it *as is* in her chest. Later policemen ask each other for stories, similar stories of trust/misdeed, and the men each recount three likely stories that happened at sundown one day on a thrilling stretch of the dusty highway from Amarillo to Houston, widened West, and the mother has clams baked in dough and the babies, they are red-faced and antagonistic.

There was 3-D exegesis going on in these regions, over-the-border transfer of primary forms, the lump of China for example curtailing forest use in Hungary from across the Rumanian border.... Mr. Jones, he-man reporter, collided with the downfall of Europe and primed his assistant for battle. "The ways of the slurping of power from out the navel of essence around these parts can be listed in twos: hitting and slapping, licking and slurping, ducking and bobbing, et cetera. Now to capture the frame for the natives of home, our own native home, flesh and its blood of our blood of our flesh, you have to duck! and bob! and generally practice the elements, remembering 'honest Pantagruel,' clearest struggle. Do you read?"

Europe was also gathering moss in the woods of Taiwan....

"Hakakakaka," cried the United States, which had the highest heart disease. "Draconian torture your lot if you do not report. If you do not spring the paling of origins from its roost in that waste of all wastes, your mind in Europe...."

Mr. Jones addressed his assistant: "The abstract behind is also your field. You glance at the tucks, the creases, the hangingest bites you can clutch in the deepest abstract behind, the deepest abstraction behind...."

The assistant writes to the chamber of men: "In a word, the one goes into the other. Fire fans fire and death goes stumbling on death, in the yard of Old Man Europe. It is more than difficult, and legend succumbs to less honest legend." The chamber of men goes wild.

There was 3-D exegesis going on in these parts, but it was behind the scenes and a long time in coming, and well-shaven old men drank coffee for years with their friends, smoking costly cigars, reading books about fear and despair, giving coins to the legless, before the world would see and buy.

JOAN OF ARC HEARD GOD, CHEMISTS PROVE

—National Enquirer, 1/31/86

There was a division of territory in the old lands at that point, and the upright stood up and down-home assassins lay low. The upright therefore became the supernal heads and the lousy warts became trash. Thus all was made right, and the division of lands was accomplished.

Mary heard a voice in her head, which commanded her to rescue the ailing admiral's fleet from the doom of the Spanish. She set out to conquer the thing, and her hard-trudging barefoot, often naked figure exultantly mastered the fields of her yesteryear, the year of her own strangers' full, proud possession of same while she'd mended the doilies, fixed the bedding, and occasionally hiked up her skirt to roam free over cotton, wheat, corn, and oat fields near cows, horses and sheep. Of forests she had been afraid.

The troops behind her were many but a different sort of thing awaited them, for the Spanish would *fix them with points*. Thus Mary's plan would be foiled and the voices winked out in the gathering dark in her eyes.

Chemists suggest a *failure of meaning*—the voices had not kept stride with the flow of events, the beings behind had vanished, emptied, stupid, vanished. But chemists are often misled, and who is to say that the people who say she was mad, or created by France, or myth out of air, are not right?

The cuisinart is again sending mass uncertainty through twenty dimensions, beginning with this. I arrive at this point, sense the cuisinart sending out mass repudiations of lingo, bang-you-up stalwartness, trees, and I feel my pulse quickening, my systems upending themselves in the struggle to keep contained, my breath getting longer and weirder.

"Hoimmm, hulnnnn, hoimmmmm, huphamnnnnnnn...."

Several of the ancient Etruscans celebrating themselves in my vestibule become my companions in those reaches of despair I always called "masturbation." I ask them what they do in their "home time." "We take care of the native plants, of the passages of great plays as yet finished, of each other in our places of joy and paternity." And what do they do for a living? "The same. Things are simple then."

They *are!* I arrest myself for the fiftieth time trying breakneck laughter as an antidote to total collaboration. With total collaboration, the problem is you don't have your own thing. You don't sit on your thing, manage your thing, divulge your thing to actual friends, ad-lib thing-hopping openly, sadly, with genius consternation. Instead you process each moment by means of the hardest tubers around, passing them in, out, in, out till the tubers or the moments become something much like butter in the abstract, and then you have beer, together, in a cubicle in a brewery, winnowing through the saddles gathering like rice in your folds, one-saddle two-saddle three-saddle four, till you all see the tautology of the little hicks licking, licking till something is all swallowed up—but there you are after all, somehow, and that's total collaboration.

Finally I allow the Etruscans into my heart and we dance openly with the ten-million-ton gay population of Coney Island as the heartfelt misanthropy of the clapboard milkmaids and postmen and gardeners comes on and tells us the truth of the thing in tones of despair. "You are suggesting nothing. In the honest glimmer of this classless moment, you eat your candor with sauce, relishing driblet, driblet, driblet. Is it the sauce? The candor? Surely not the candor, because I have seen more candid by far, and I am only the working people's misanthropy."

The Etruscans wave goodbye. How can they? I look around for the cuisinarts, always hidden as per tradition in layers of service, utility, genius. O genius! that hides a cuisinart in itself as do service, utility. O manifold genius, as much so as cuisinarts in each species and rendering. I do not disdain it. I look for it and find it, and there are the cuisinarts. There they are, and the mass uncertainty wending through fifty dimensions calms down at my look, betrothes itself to the castle by the water, hungers there after split dragon *mole*, relates to itself finally in a breakthrough of character advance.

I, in my room, snap up some loose information and stick to my guns with it. I cannot do otherwise. When information is as good as this, the earnestness of my approach builds on itself and eventually all are happy.

Paracelsus was admonishing the energetic divers to beware the explosions that could signal demise of the great underwater city, because then they must escape quickly to not be prey to the horrors that would surely come to the surroundings. The divers were listening carefully, half engrossed in their own thoughts about the great underwater city—What were its streets like? How about its hotels? Were there prostitutes?

There were indeed some prostitutes, as diver Mike found out. Large ones, with great horned pates, and all male: not much to his liking. He eddied about in the great underwater city, furthering too his interests by jackknifing from one spot of some interest to the next and eyeballing each passing mongrel of the deep.

But then the city exploded as Paracelsus had warned, and Mike had time only to think of his buddy Alf, who was perched on a rock far away in the Mediterranean getting his bum buzzed pleasantly by the Rock of Gibraltar. The earthquake was "the pleasant one" of 1992, and that was that.

Alf meandered into the tiny hub of commercial activity so uncharacteristic of the surface of the Mediterranean, punctuated here by the hardness of the Rock of Gibraltar and allowing, for example, a bit of commercial activity including sock repairing, boot matching, and cortisone-injection trading: a shop or two for each, each with its friendly, large-knobbed face, ghastly cheek-points a point of advantage and beauty here on the Rock of Gibraltar, in contradistinction to their aspect elsewhere in the world.

Alf did a thing or two with some cortisone for his buddy Mike, with whom he had "exported casks." He thought, "This ought to get him." But Mike was virtually nothing now; in fact a bit of Mike was washing up onto the beach that Alf had slept on the night before, a chunklet that Alf would soon rub through his hair, thinking "deep, deep" for no particular reason.

Kim, in Idaho, was tending crops with a verve that gave his uncle a chill of joy, for he knew that in this boy's hands the farm would expand to the economic limits of the Valley Duchesne, sending power and glory abroad for their fair distribution by naked women of every concern and practice, no matter how bewildering.

Kim's uncle was daydreaming of a great underwater city and a young man named Mike, the sometime needful lover of a young man named Alf, and their horrible experience with the death of Mike in the great underwater city whose base-rocking final explosions had been predicted by Paracelsus, who at this point, as luck would have it, was trudging severely across the vastnesses and relevances of the Idaho scenery, further, further, closer to Kim's uncle and Kim, who now was the first to see him—"There, uncle! There is the trudging, energetic figure of a sage!"

"You are right, nephew: there is a sage."

"I am very interested in buying some radishes," Paracelsus said in a high, raspy voice.

"Next farm," Kim and Kim's uncle said in unison, and sent Paracelsus off down the road with some friendly glances and a barrelful of good tidings for their neighbor, the friendly radish farmer.

Eating the food was the least part. Eighty Chinese attracted him to the Gate of Cats where he saw a gruesome display by some men. The food was good, all the same. Rarebit and stockade rice was one dish known by a different name to the people around him. He didn't use chopsticks. The things he could buy were too numerous to mention. "Lose yourself," the merchants said. "Don't worry about price or misfortune. In the provinces they refer to us as men of no difficulty."

Later he succumbed to the charms of the Prime Minister. The Prime Minister invited him to his mansion by the highway and treated him to boys, first, then girls, then Chinese soda-pop from the province of T. The large man understood that to take the gifts was rude. Finally he saw a movie by the premier Chinese movie director, Sergio B.

The way home involved an expenditure of effort by S. K. R. in Geneva and Q. N. in New York.

A Gigantic Yet Soaring, Hurtling Plan of the Previous Men's Devising

> Aeneas watched the progress of the assault upon the palace from the top of certain lofty roofs, to which he ascended for the purpose.... This tower Aeneas and the Trojans who were with him contrived to cut off at its base, and throw over upon the throngs of Grecians that were thundering.... Great numbers were killed by the falling ruins, and the tortoise was broken down.
>
> —Jacob Abbott, *History of Romulus*, 1854

First there were thousands, unruly thousands lining the boulevards, then a few dozen encouraged some stragglers to join in the fray, then there was ruckus as Aeneas, a real surround of magnificent blossoms of hot-to-trot courage, shot ardent, consoling glances at Shipshape, one of the recent stragglers, a canvas-covered lad of an overall sullen neighboring tribe.

Shipshape, telepathically: "I want to understand the way you dominate us and helm such a civilization as yours, Aeneas, which I understand is a mighty civilization in which we all participate as equal and present partners. My heritage is neither important enough nor slipping so much that I need to save it—not like a palaceful of gilt yarn over the edge of the sea, nor like someone screaming for help lashed to a chair gurgling comically towards the end of a river. No! Instead, I can gaze in a dry, even way, with mirth, even, into the eyes of Aeneas, wondering, 'How might it be that together, he and I could more widely undo the hosts of the wicked?'"

Aeneas, telepathically: "It is not often that I am so struck by one such as this, this cloth-covered lad, and in so uncontrollably open a way that I might invite doom, being a leader of men who depends for his strength on the esteem of the giant, grunting, deciduous monsters that are men of my tribe, which is a terrible tribe from up north, full of swearing, buss-cocking fucks in pyjamas, or pelts that look like pyjamas (and are often used thus on the streets of metropolises, so I hear, where the fad is to wear pyjamas even in the

137

leavening-pits of the corners).... No, this is not a love to pass up, but is a dangerous, enjoyable love instead. Here, Shipshape (for that is your name), give me your hand."

Shipshape races up, knocking men over, and there amidst the thousands, Aeneas and Shipshape join hands and perch on the same ox to the catcalls of the boors of Aeneas's tribe that Aeneas suddenly realizes he's free from, his base of support being much wider now: he thumbs his nose, he wiggles his tongue, he bats at his Adam's apple and adjures the boors to envision highrises over their mothers' plots, may the plots sink a foot. Shipshape lounges categorically, without loss of a beat, upon the great shoulder, which gives a bit at the seam with the chest, which disappoints young Shipshape, who imagined a starker physiognomy to such grandeur. But he is soon overwhelmed with an epic, which noses its way into his mind as was the wont of epics of yore, before the boundary between epics and the minds of dummies was drawn in stone. For a while he stares into space, illiterate.

"Hello," the two call out in synchrony to the crowd, which waves in synchrony too, grand pattern, waving fleshtone plains, "hello." It is amazing how loud the two call, amazing the synchrony of the crowd. Suddenly the national history vanishes. Suddenly the purpose of the epic they belong to, the *Aeneid*, asserts itself in the air, great, cold, glassy truth: its purpose is to be pretty, itself and everything in it, which is everything. The crowd, the lovers, the air itself attempt to convey to the audiences they know will be theirs just how beautiful everything is, without aid, without work, without error-strewn wreaking on the part of the nations whose survival or lack of it leaves them quite cold.

A boy in Virginia hears them, looks up from his *History of Romulus* and farts. The master administers whacks with a ferule, the boy's knuckles are bruised and the difficulty of living in such contradiction impels him to die, whereupon he's reborn as a shack in Milwaukee, exposed to the sun after "Plump," the mulberry shade tree, is cut for the neighbors' view. The neighbors are nazis.

Many, similarly, are the sad and painful truths endured by all the peoples of earth thereafter on account of this hero and that non-hero, but ever so often the love of Shipshape and Aeneas arises and smarts in the wings of an ineffectual tyranny. There are many who would call this the effect of chance, or ill-defined patterns of action (or even patterns of chaos), but in fact it is all trigonometry.

THEY LIVED TOO TRITELY

I have heard it went well, this latest of the Excesses of the Sodomites, with the ice cream barely melting, and everyone going home full and fiery.

The answer this time was "Poe-tree emotion," therefore "Poetry in motion," and that pleased everyone.

Not me. Not Brian. Not Nkeithi.

This was the fourth of the week's Excesses, so no one complained that it lasted but an hour.

This has been a good week!

Not for me. Not for Brian. Not for thoughtful, wealthy Nkeithi.

Nkeithi just looks at the ceiling. She's got an obsession with cracks, thinks there's something about them. "Random yet obtuse," she calls them. "Leaks in the dome," she calls them.

"My aching heart throbs only for you," I tell her.

The Excesses of the Sodomites was a record last week, for someone had delivered "Causation" by means of "Caw, Alsacian— La!" The entourage was stunned because of obscurity. But also because of opacity. The discoverer was the twin of the wit, and they bought a crate. Donatelli's Joy. Red fudge.

"I would give you a thousand crates," I tell Nkeithi. She is fair and has eyelids a little too large for her eyes, just perfect. Neither of us has ever discovered a pun. That is dangerous, but we aren't concerned. We are perfectly at ease, and completely uneasy. We love each other and the bloom of our lips.

It is only the passion that stands in our way. I am fatally attracted to these gatherings, these ridiculous scurryings of townsfolk, when we stand near each other, we townsfolk, and reminisce, and figure things out, yea slew upon slew of things, and we don't even question the future elucidation of yet more things....

"Truth and devices," Nkeithi mutters, swatting at a fly. "They confuse them! Truth is what you have that is pretty real, and devices is everything else. The difference between, say, knowing Bernard's pretence and, say, knowing that Bernard pretends." Her visage is cloudy but is just starting to lighten. Instinctively I try to keep her rolling.

"But everyone devises," I say. "Every wit, at the least."

"And a wit is the one who will found and founder, eh? The wit is the daring yakker? A clown with a bag?" Nkeithi turns over to face the wall. She is not bugged, though. This is odd. I try not to appreciate her quick curves but to watch all the walls for reflections—a shadow might keep me posted.

"Well all right," I finally say. "Maybe it's a big waste of time. Maybe it's a big fucking cruel, wasteful, ill-rigged state of meanness. Maybe it's the biggest miser fucking the stupidest corn farmer in the world. Maybe we're out of *rights*. Out of *employment*."

"Damn," Nkeithi mutters, shifting herself slightly. *What is she doing?*

"And maybe it's a big darling waste. All those wits a-parading their efforts, just looking up and down, checking out the townsfolk, pretending to be insight, true meaning...." I can feel her head brighten. I egg her on. "Well maybe you have it. Maybe you're right. But honey, if we didn't have wits...."

Suddenly Nkeithi is on her back and looking right at me with pain in her eyes. She puts a hand on her lower back. I ask if she's all right, but she just turns back to the wall. Strange.... I press on.

"Um, listen honey, there's nothing wrong with devices. I mean if you didn't have devices, what would you do? Where's the fault? It doesn't impede. It doesn't sniffle at all the wrong moments, so to speak. A wit..."

Nkeithi now screams. I get hit; I grab her back and she smiles. And now, I can feel it.

A crick.

At "A wit."

Obvious keys.

A crick.

A wit.

The keys.

A crick.

Shaw.

Keys.

I tilt my head and put my foot on the bed, smiling wide. Nkeithi sits up, smiling wide. I lay my hand on her head and smile so wide it hurts my eyes. Nkeithi's face tilts to the right. I speak.

"A crick—Shaw keys. A rickshaw ease. We are."

Nkeithi takes my hand and we make mad nudity all over the bed. And then we leave. "We will take them by storm," she says. "Why didn't we think of this earlier?" I say. "Why hasn't anyone else?" she says. "Maybe it's too difficult." "This does beat 'Causation.'" "It beats everything," I say. "There's no way we can go wrong."

And we don't. We do a little waltz by Donatelli, the Red Deliverer waltz, and bring tubs and tubs of ice cream, too much, and the townsfolk get a little jittery from the sugar, and we're all dressed up and correct but they can tell something's wrong, they can tell we've got a finger on the pilot light, and they all go slack in the face as we say it.... They've got our message, they're stunned.... They'd lynch us if they weren't so intelligent....

They look at us, look at us, look at us. The atmosphere has certainly soured. A sturdy young man looks at us sourly and speaks, resentfully.

"From across the bold-streaming waters.

"In China there was Wu Liang. He owned a buggy with a little man that ran it and every day he made it to go get the people, in it they rode. A thousand days. Thousands of men and ladies.

"Ouch! The man is dead! He lies clawing at dirt in clutching-up of his muscles. 'Oh,' says Wu Liang. 'All this time I have been enjoying the life and the puller of my buggy is dead. I think there is too much triteness in the common life. The life of the people is more of worth than to be pulled about by a dying man. There surely is more!'"

Nkeithi and I go home to contemplate things, like whether or not we've done any good, and where's Brian, and how come a town can understand a critique of three words so well they get stunned and hyperbolic.

"Maybe they're not so bad after all," one of us says, nudging the other, taking in the stars, kicking the dew, and hoping for joy, joy, joy.

I Am a Normal Graduate Student But Then I Fall into the Hands of the Turks, Who Show Me Some Kindness

I used to like to butcher texts pretty bad so it wasn't a real dastardly thing to do to wrap me up in a sheet and shut me up in a trunk and surrender me to the Turks the way Bill did that hot full-moon night that we swooned with each other next to the river hard by the school we attended.

I got mad, still and all, and in spite I upset the Turks' notions of autodidacticism by proving that though I had learned all I knew by myself, I was cruel, snide and prudish. The Turks, and by power of suggestion all Turks, fell into a contemplative stupor from which they recovered only in the next phase of their civilization, upon which by marrow-deep reflex they showered me with a sticky stuff that coated my pores so my skin couldn't breathe anymore and I froze up all stiff-jointed, mad, and the Turks got behind their munitions and begged me for forgiveness for everything they'd done to me so far, and I offered it to them gaily and fast on the condition they take care to find some butane or what-not and clean my skin of the sticky stuff, which turned out to be the actual condensed blood of all of their great Turkish prophets (which naturally upset them some too, and they recounted at length the story of their prophets, which turned out to be quite unusual).

Here is the text of my statement to these Turks the next day, in which I explain where I came from. It shows that though of poor stock, I am kind, martial and pithy (a fact the Turks found simple to celebrate):

> Is aught the beam of sturgeons' clip
> on sea, that nape of dripping lamb—
> or mirth the cantilever's sashay
> creaming sham pâté, aghast?

That was nothing! Here is the text of my statement to the Turks the week after, as many of us were traversing the Caspian Sea in search of sellable notions:

> Here is the vast
> uproarious slat

in greed—
mead, our sole bond

Perhaps, one of them said, you are needing a whiff of the
stridency of the Turkish choirs which stipple Constantinople with
boy-charm. Perhaps that would arch your contrition and limber
your strut. Here is part of the text I spoke in response, though the
paper for the whole would swallow ten North Americas:

> Gunning to valleys succinctly lined on the charts of
>   the greatest of latter-day wanderers
> I and you and the host of fungi and one-celled attached
>   assist the general dimple we've sunk in the blue
> This is not less than the growth on a brother's shoulder
> This is not less than the cursive of somebody's first-
>   grader damning a kitchen
> This is tremendous!
> How many traders would smile?

I accepted, there on the sea, preferring the voice of a boy to that
of a fish any old day, and we changed our course (laden as we were
with a nation's wealth of golden teacups due in Kentucky) towards
Constantinople, where indeed there were many fine choirs with
many fine boys and the rest is contained in the annals I laid down
through my scribes (I illiterate). They are called *Dear Bill* after the
youth who abandoned me to the Turks so long before they and I
learned to speak in distinct but unruly patterns across the cultural
gulfs that kept us forever apart.

THE DEATH OF KILIMANJARO
Mountains

There was a time when your average man didn't know about mountains. He was middle-aged and tired, worn down from the boss who was mountains and mountains bigger than him in many important respects, and he didn't know about mountains. He knew about coke and caffeine and the medleys they play at sports events, and death in the jungle and death on the sideboard and death at various sports events, and Christchurch and Scotland and even Kilimanjaro, but blow us all to heaven if he knew about the mountains involved, if he knew about the way you can regulate your fires using a mountain, chastise your relatives using a mountain, forget important appointments using a mountain. He didn't know a thing!

So when your average man went to Kenya, looking for weevils and other exotica advertised in *Bad News Okay*, he wasn't looking at mountains. He wasn't going to be standing in various flatlands, looking at mountains. Nor climbing those mountains. Nor looking up close for a claimant to the mountain failing which he would take the mountain himself, at least for the week. Your average man was in Northern Tanzanian boutiques combing fleas from his hair onto chinoiseries, buying scrap and soap, lounging in chairs from the dynasties, eating the cookies and soups there offered. He was chasing the girls and boys away from his brocade pouch. He was lathering up and reading the gloss on African hostage events, and hoping for luck with the madman, Charles, and lunching at Billboard Finesse, and hoarding his rare sanity against stock futures.

That is why we know nothing about the death of Kilimanjaro, except that it involved the waylaying of several important personages from the routes they were accustomed to following home in the cool summer dusk after the twenty-four-hour housefly dies, and that it was enormous and left these several important personages buried in ash for a good ten centuries. And that is why we will invent its death, put it on the table of everyone's kitchen as if it were known, and ten years from now no one will know the difference. The wife will come home and see Kilimanjaro as if it were yesterday, the husband and children will romp and decide things, large-scale guests will sit at the window and chew, chew, chew, as they glean the last droplets of talk about Kilimanjaro from slow passers-by—everything will have happened there as we have predicted, and it will have always been so.

Boy Enters Palace, Envisions Problem, Improves

I wouldn't have known what to do with such an attractive part of the world swimming around in a tub owned in part by the Duchess. Fortunately the Duchess came in and seized the attractive part of the world and made it her own, to match the tub in that quality.

How I got into the royal palace is odd. I know I was there, and it had something to do with the pavement, contortions or swoons (I am cheesy, but after all the pavement reared up)—I must have effectively swum right in through one of the holes in the palace that weren't intended for land dwellers' entrance or absence of same: delivered myself, just made myself part and parcel of a systematic bereavement of morals by age without the requisite training in strength against untoward visions. (Perceived thus as a danger I limped around softly—but the Duchess is known for her sensitivity.)

The bathtub was splendid and apparently filled with the Duchess's taste, so I guessed it was something to do with the Duchess, perhaps linked by ownership, even. I was right. It is not very often I find myself downed by a bathtub, but I hardly stood in place without swimming about, and things turned green and blue and finally black.

When I awoke the bathtub was in its last-mentioned state, filled by a very attractive part of the world, obviously of some rank or other (who wasn't?), sudsing herself in a way that signalled a talent for just about everything, mostly things I could hardly imagine—such laving in the heart of cowardice, it suddenly occurred to me, for I hated the palace.

There was more, but of course the Duchess, large as always in the public eye (which now happened to be just my own), came attending her morsel and I was caught with attentions in all the wrong places and, caught off guard, I was regaled with certain things' happening in orders I didn't quite know.

The hole I got to know was twenty feet wide and contained about thirty other fellows of some distinction and yet not quite so much as my own, and they thought me so odd as to agree to relinquishing rights to a decent burial in many lands until one night the Duchess herself descended in purple as thick as doom, and she opened a discourse on tragedy which ended with a tiny treatise on dwarves: "And proper to them is liquidity."

146

Many somewhat attractive things got thought thereafter, as I learned from a series of actions upon my person that left me spellbound by something akin to eternity hovering above and to the left of me in the freakish pink darkness of my relative solitude. I call them "attractive" because of the nature of us, the sort of rope we are heaved by, the coin of our slide.

Now I believe only in the supreme terrific principles known here and there by names unrepeatable, believed by people in darkening corners of famous cities here and abroad, a great, taut knowing that it feels rather pleasant to dwell in.

There are other methods of knowing—and by the way, I am free, now, roaming the places, not in a cell with the many distinct, no longer a boy but certainly vague and vital—and I have explored them all: the method of swagger-and-sup, the method of Turkestan Abrightening, the method of daze. But there is a difference. I am very aware of a difference.

When I think of the Duchess's bathtub and things plowing down my attention and life going on in manifold swoons to the parquet, I laugh and men see me laughing and I must explain myself with a frown and a constellation of brooding abutted by books. That is not so unpleasant, but there are better ways to remain out of glances, such as being of different stock, not human. But that will not happen, and the things I know are forever, and nothing will stop me from laughing, and effort is no great mustard.

Breakfast was serene and I ventured forth to unearth some pastures from below the dirt that had accumulated over the centuries since Sadie had arrived from the far ends of the earth and dined and enjoyed some time and breakfasted now, and the pastures were fairly okay and I put some cow dung down and some people surrounded me and that was okay and I went back and lunched on some food.

There was something really intense, he noticed. Something very wild about the way the things worked, the way the one moved over, the thing happened, seven times thirty would be your Trafalgar, sixteen thugs in a browning sauce over E-Z, super class, super mass, everything chancing itself on a throw of the moratorium—how he loved the thing, eventually, after he had spent a good month in noticing it.

The thing he loved was awesome. It had the total breadth of a great many love things. Many attunements, total, containing the stealth and meringue of a great tongue. Many things happening all at once.

He would go to the cocktail parties.

His eyes were extremely wide and his skin was sagging and there was something totally bald about his head. How could he know about Liechtenstein? How could he laugh on the phone, divulging the secret for which you could destine him to slapstick? How could you ignore his body, however hideous, when he might notice your rejection before it happened, start seeing in you the seeds of your own importance, and grant you that way a real animated humanity you might not sell for anything?

Addictive behavior? Addictive behavior is that which continues itself—the French republic, for example. The French republic is that which is ruled by the French *en masse*.

Was it addictive of him to go to the places he went and enjoy talking up and down the length of the very entrancing madmen who frequented such places, drink in hand, mastery underfoot? The erotic madmen, was it addictive of him to have them all to himself in the parlor? If so, whom precisely was it addicting? Not the madmen?

I, for example, was confronted with him, and I enjoyed his bug-eyes and though he was cute I found him not cute, but though I found him not cute I wanted to do him, and though I wanted to do him I couldn't and there wasn't the time and he showed me out the door and he was happy and his roommate was not. His roommate, obviously enough, had had the same life as he had and failed.

All of these things—and that he has made me think about him as if he were Warhol—wrench from me blessings or gratitude or whatever it is they get warmed by.

He himself was not warmed by me, since I left after he'd taken down my number.

If I had stayed and he had wanted me to stay, things would have taken their course and there would have been some frightfully intimate sex and I would have forgotten him sooner than I have. Instead there is only autonomy. I am lost today; I have newly discerned the matter of dating as something to do with me—I am no longer obligated to have just now found the boy-cum-old-man of my dreams, and am freed from the wallops of stiff breads and leather.

There are several things I am thankful for, and one of them is that I can still get disturbed and not fall off the edge of my sanctity. If I were to fall off the edge of just about anything to do with me, I would be speechless, and I am constantly challenging myself to be speechless, running at cliffs. When I go to the synagogue I get sudden rushes of a very great madness as well as a gradual swell. There is speech there, the basis of speech; its basis is speech.

Is it addictive behavior to know what is going on at every moment, or to tell someone's life before he has opened his book?

HERE WE ARE AGAIN

I, as one member of the tremendous Twenty-Four-Gun-Salute team called Joy Riff-Raff of Connecticut, was inclined to view death, its concomitants and advocates, and the smell associated with death as vile, treacherous enemies likely to get you when you're in the rough, which is to say as we all in the Twenty-Four-Gun-Salute team Joy Riff-Raff of Connecticut were.

The story behind this may never be fully told, as there are many other stories which must be told first. It is even impossible to explain why we were in the rough, or what being in the rough really meant (in relation to diamonds? golfballs?). The number of other stories which must be told first is enormous, and the tale of death is trivial—trivial! to the point of needing only the words of skin flux to describe it.

So listen to the stories, which will skirt, of course, the story of our group and its name and its feelings about that big fiend, death.

The first story is about a bad man, Hubert. Hubert had some angina, left of pimple. Left of the pimple! we had noticed fifteen years ago at a cook-out, nude in the forest clearing, romantically unbangled, saying "There! There is the pimple we have known in our dreams. There!"

Hubert had been none too amused. At that point he had left our group. It was only through strangers, stranger upon loathsome stranger, that we heard now about his bit of angina, his modicum of death-palaver, his trifling bump-up against middling Señor Muerte of the "two-bit consumerism diversion habits."

Muriel, another bad person in another story, another ex-member, had just now involved her hair in some vats of true misery, lynched her own blueprint that way, yes, we had heard; this one, she had left us oh twenty years back in a season of no lack of flurries, flurry flurry here and flurry flurry from the top of your hairdo—note the connection! Muriel, shit in the greening wind of true romance, was mastering the art of noticing hair in the glass.

True Muriel!

Murphy, on the other hand, a good man in yet another story, didn't care. Murphy could sit fifty years on a fence balancing buns with a chest of fine dish-shaped muscles, full fifty years and still not sop up reindeer mufflings with that cowardly antenna you can sometimes see poking up out of the ears of folk too long sitting on fences, shiftier folk than Murphy, of course.... No, Murphy was God's own pip in the earnestness of all our afflictions. All our afflictions. All.

You see, so far, about our group, through these stories: we have a varied group; in time we are varied; in allegiance to group and containment in group we are varied (Murphy at one end, Muriel and Hubert at the other); in readability our fortunes are varied, for some of us are settled and free (Murphy), regardless of vile existences matching their klutziness to our heat (Hubert and Muriel), while others (Hubert and Muriel) are prodded to unseeable acts (Hubert and Muriel) by the tiny of fault (Murphy) in order that the world as a whole, mysteriously and to the doom of the wrong (Hubert and Muriel), might prosper.

You can see, more importantly, that there are many stories to be told besides the story of our name and death-orientation and so on, a story others tell only through totally misguided but admittedly wonderfully herculean efforts. So watch, and listen, and soon you will grow the most magnificent pair of be-bop kaftans upon your twin bonces, causing the envy of all New York's effortless children, making the very sun turn a jewelly way.

HOW THE FISH MERCHANT TURNED OUT OKAY
Trolls, Dreams, Adaptations

The fish merchant was eighty feet high. That made it difficult for little three-foot people (everyone else) to come purchase fish from him, even though they had the correct change (in the shape of porcupines, a famous disease and rice).

Little three-foot (-like-everyone-else) Ollie one day decided to conquer the eighty-foot fish merchant. He bought a lot of fish from the ocean, from the table the ocean had laid out by the lip of the ocean, and put it in a big tower called Gus which turned out in fact to be a very unhappy raging land-walker of a tower which chose now, a volume of fish its core, to go stalking about the countryside ravaging this, ravaging that, till there were plates so clean you couldn't call your gods with their crumbs lest the gods start screaming "What?! You couldn't muster some volumes and volumes of crumbs like I like?!" and the people have to run like palsied newcomers all over that journey-ridden domain.

But of course the people were running like palsied newcomers all over that journey-ridden domain and had no time to sacrifice anyhow, and needn't have worried about licking their plates so clean on the run, except that that was their habitus, to go from staid little energetics in the constant purchase of fish to great roaring worry-warts three feet high.

Poor, sad tiny folk!

Awful, rictally noticeable giant in the incorrect vending of fish!

Ollie was successful. The terrible tower, Gus, became much more docile when Ollie launched himself via catapult across the domain and smashed into the tower, stopping it and producing from it the first pillow, which the fish merchant did lay his head down on, sleeping.

In the course of his sleep the fish merchant dreamt of a great russet hawk named Alphonse who was actually a preternatural kingdom of starlets and pleasant blue goblets that all consulted on the problem of diminution of the national moods. "Lesser moods," cried an Alphonsian starlet: "they are our pressing burden, huge, unpleasant, cleansing our blasphemies into pattern-rhymes, making it seem like dough when the clipper ships feint Masses to keep the sardines running—shit of lessening! Is it real?" "It is not!"

cried a pleasant blue goblet of Alphonse. "It is only a taste of the wide blue flip!" In this dream the hawk flew into the sun, aiding it considerably.

In the morning the fish merchant understood: his attitude should be one of short-native abetment, and he remained prone while his world flew and his little friends of awesome purchasing ability amassed a cosmos of very interesting mood-swings, which was a good thing because there was joy in there, and cosmos-dusting pain, and patterns of justifiable glassy-eyedness that did not alarm either the fish merchant or anyone else because all understood that important aspect of self which involves a look inward that may last through several concerts, meals and even diseases.

The cars started bouncing up and down on the road. The people crossed the street and their heads spun in circles, around and around their necks. The buildings swayed back and forth, their windows bulging forth in great snaky blobs, their chimneys blaring forth "Dawn of the Dust." Assyrians crushed into the city from the south, their chests exploding, imploding, exploding. Vermin streaked across the sky, spelling "DREDGE THE SLAPSTICK." Little gray foxes made up tacky minuets in all the parking lots, annoying the men who scraped their enormous teeth across the asphalt while chanting with their sphincters.

Mark arrived and declared that war was a gone idea. His teeth were brittle and green and his nose was five inches wide and its nostrils were flapping so fast that he acquired about an inch of loft per second. Within a year he would be beyond the atmosphere, and his teeth would be out and poisoning the atmosphere so that everyone would gasp and stutter.

A troop of boy scouts arrived to help Mark cross himself. Three of the scouts, on a slowly rising ball of froth, lifted his right arm at the elbow; another sat on his hand to lower it to his forehead; one of the three let go and the hand went down to Mark's chest; that one pushed up again and a fifth pushed left, then right. Someone got in Mark's mouth and said "Domini, Domini, Domini" all the while Mark was saying that war "will cripple our various industries and plunge us into a bad sort of process re: basic services."

A great swinish woman suddenly went totally flat, rotated onto her side, flew out the window and onto the street, and started screaming like an electric saw as she cut a great slice down the yellow divider for sixteen blocks, lopping the left fender from a good number of cars. Kids scurried out to collect them. The woman, recomposed, apologized to the peace officer who assured her this was nothing a pub couldn't fix; together they built one but staffed it with guinea pigs by mistake, and many a beer went unswigged.

The atmosphere, preparing itself for Mark's teeth, wrapped itself in the remains of the city and coughed out great undulating fishbowls. Its dusky features appealed to many caught in one fold or other, and they drew them wherever they could find a piece of chalk and a surface. Mark continued to rise, describing the formidable lapses sure to occur any time now, admiring the atmosphere's taking in hand of events. The principle thing about himself, he noted, was that he had no personality. The unusual physical aspects of his existence were nothing to that. Many a creature could rise to the exits of the earth and poison worlds, but it would be a find were one utterly bland like he was. He was a find, he decided. Perhaps this would make him valuable, and give him a group of people to admonish, which, he believed, would make him happy.

A vastness of raccoons many and unresolvable crept through the fabric of reality, entering this or that mind, bathroom, or textbook at this or that moment. Mark found this exciting, and began to speak about it. "Perhaps this tide of raccoons, this no small gushet of raccoons, will enhance our discrepant objectivities till they meld in spite of themselves."

HORTATORY INDEX

A

Abdomens 58, 72, 110
Aeneid 58, 138
American imperialism 13, 19, 32, 42, 67, 101, 119
Androgyny, usefulness of 24
Angora cats, discourses aimed at 103
Annelids 38
Apocalypse 21, 30, 68, 81
Arizona 13, 86
Art history 113
Assyrians 154
Autodidacticism, false beauty of 142

B

Baldessari, John 109
Barbarian boys 18, 54, 75, 137
Basic services 154
Baton Rouge 91
Biosphere 13
Birds 11, 17, 71, 77, 114
Blake, William 37
Boy scouts, religious fervor and 154
Bug-eyes, attractiveness of 148
Buttocks 67, 110

C

Caravaggio 34
Cartography, eighteenth-century 30
Char, René 17
Chemists 131
Chinese cinema 136
Christo 109
Cleopatra 123
Colorado 109
Constellations, Southern 87